"In a time when the importance of teachers has been unfairly challenged, Bob Boone gives us a collection of simply told, hard-edged tales from the lives of educators and their students. These rich, multifaceted stories ring true with details gleaned over the course of a full life. Reading them, one feels as if they are entering another version of our familiar reality, where secrets thrive in quiet classrooms and a passionate love of the pitfalls and victories of teaching motivates the creation of narrative."

—Lisa Locascio, University of Southern California
Recipient of the 2011 John Steinbeck Award for Fiction

"These aren't your typical teacher stories. In the living and breathing world of brick, glass and glue sticks, we want our teachers to leave their real lives—their darknesses, their longings, their secrets and desires—back at their desks and locked in their lockers in the faculty room. But this is Bob Boone's school. There is no safe place here for the containment of these things. The best Boone's characters can do is take off their jackets at the door, empty the pockets of their pants—their shreds and crumplings, their histories and regret, their hearts and longings—stuff it all in the pockets and sleeves of their jackets, drape their coats over the backs of their chairs, and just like the rest of us, cross their fingers and pray to God that nothing falls out before the bell rings."

—Billy Lombardo, Author, *The Man with Two Arms*
Recipient of the 2011 Nelson Algren Award for the Short Story

D1446004

"Implicit in these tales are basic human questions: what does it mean to be a good teacher or a good person? What, for that matter, is meant by the phrase 'good school'? In this age of standardized tests and the relentless attempt at quantifying students and teachers alike, Bob's stories offer a refreshingly human portrayal of his characters. He never fails to see the comedy in the conflict between the conventional and unconventional, and he portrays his characters with nothing less than a sympathetic eye. In these stories, Bob always looks beyond the Forest to the individual trees."

—John O'Connor, Author, *Wordplaygrounds*
Teacher at New Trier High School

"Bob Boone gives us an insider's view into the world of Forest High. These stories are spare, terse and capture the quirkiness of characters and circumstance utterly consistent with the world of schools—a world where, as Boone well knows, every story implies another. An astute observer, Bob Boone writes with humor, compassion and insight."

—Larry Starzec, Fiction Editor, *Willow Review*
Professor of English at College of Lake County

"The stories are wonderful and beautifully written, with insights into the interior of a parallel, minimalist universe of the everyday. What makes these stories ultimately so arresting is how they capture the quiet, unspoken fears, the normalcy of unfinished relationships, and the inner strength it takes to face each day. The quietness of the stories belies their energy and the resilience of the characters which becomes a moving celebration of the human spirit.

—Milos Stehlik, Critic for Worldview
on WBEZ/Chicago Public Radio

BOOKS BY BOB BOONE

Back to Forest High
Amika Press

Write Through Chicago
With Mark Henry Larson
Amika Press

Forest High
Amika Press

Joan's Junk Shop
With Mark Henry Larson
Good Year Books

Moe's Cafe
With Mark Henry Larson
Good Year Books

Inside Job: A Life of Teaching
Puddin'head Press

Developing Your Test-Taking Skills
National Textbook Company

Language and Literature
Ed., McDougal Littell, Inc

Verbal Review and Workbook for the SAT
Harcourt Brace Jovanovich Publishers

Hack
Follett Publishing Company

Using Media
Peacock Press

Back to Forest High

stories by Bob Boone

"Coach" first appeared in *Confluence* © 2000
"Funny in the Summer" first appeared in *New Scriptor* © 2009
"The Caddy" first appeared in *Forest High* © 2011

First Edition   ISBN 13: 978-1-937484-38-5

AMIKA PRESS   53 W Jackson BLVD 660 Chicago IL 60604
847 920 8084   info@amikapress.com
Available for purchase on amikapress.com

Edited by Ann Wambach & Amy Sawyer. Cover photography by Dean Terry. Author photography by Sue Boone. Designed & typeset by Sarah Koz. Set in Garamond Premier Pro, designed by Claude Garamond in the mid-1500s, digitized by Robert Slimbach in 2005–07. Thanks to Nathan Matteson.

For Sue

Contents

Introduction

I wrote a teaching memoir titled *Inside Job* in 2000. In it, I told the story of how I grew from a traditional English teacher working in Staten Island, New York, into a more radical teacher working all over the place. The title referred to my gradual realization that I was at my best when I encouraged my students to discover their unique strengths and then put those strengths to good use. This was hardly a new idea, but it was new to me and led me to a life devoted to creative writing.

I enjoyed writing *Inside Job,* and teachers in particular

liked reading it. I wanted to keep writing about schools, but I didn't want to be restricted to what had actually happened to me. Instead, I wanted to choose the narrator. I wanted to decide how much the narrator would know. I wanted to shape characters and situations into complete, credible stories. In other words, I wanted to write fiction.

Forest High, a book of nine short stories, was my first book of fiction. It features rookie teachers, seasoned teachers, struggling teachers, misunderstood teachers, irresponsible teachers, and true teachers. It also tells of motivated students, barely motivated students, cruel students, and compassionate students. The stories happen in school, after school, near school, and far from school and usually involve people facing problems—often of their own making—and trying to come up with solutions. Some characters succeed; many do not.

The reviews were positive, especially from teachers, who thought I exposed a side of teaching that only fiction could reveal.

Back to Forest High is more school fiction. Again by using imagination and memory I have tried to create stories that take advantage of fiction's power to explore singular moments.   —*Bob Boone*

Ruben's
Career Move

Her name was Alice. She looked to be in her forties—slim and serious. She looked like she didn't need to smile. She was there at that first meeting in the late summer and nodded politely when Ruben introduced himself to the other English teachers. She listened while he explained to the group that he had tired of life as an editor, but not of work. He had always wanted to teach, and now he could do it. He was the new fifty-five-year-old kid on the block.

She had looked at him extra hard that first day. The others smiled agreeably, but she had looked hard and frowned. He was sure she was going to ask a question, but she didn't.

That first night there was an English department gathering at O'Reilly's. Ruben was told that Ben, the department chairman, always had these parties. This year Ben gave out T-shirts. On each was printed: "Watch where you dangle your modifier."

Ruben was never alone that night. The teachers asked predictable questions, and he gave the same answers. He had tired of work with the publishing company. He had left under good terms. He entered a graduate program for returning executives. He got good grades. And now here he was, drinking with his new colleagues. Some of these teachers were about his age, but most were a little younger and some a lot younger.

Toward the end of the evening, Ben stood up on the bar and clapped for attention. He looked about forty years old. Young to be the department head. He wore shorts and a Hawaiian shirt and had an earring. He smiled easily and looked totally relaxed in front of his teachers, who hollered at him in a good-natured, half-drunken way. He could have handled a press conference for a politician. "I am here," he shouted, "to give you the acronym of the year. Are you all ready?" After more guffawing and groaning from the crowd, he waved them quiet. "The word for this year is— ta-da—SWARM. Each letter stands for a key word. A teaching word." More shouting and guffawing. But he pressed on, "S stands for savor as much as you can, W stands for watch for opportunities, A is ask good questions, R is for relax when you can, M is motivate. You got that? SWARM." More agreeable grumbling and shouting and finally loud applause.

Ben bowed and then leaped to the floor. Ruben stood in the back. He couldn't help smiling. He couldn't decide if the guy was a lovable fool or something more, but he liked him. He definitely liked him. Just then, he felt someone grab his arm. It was Alice, who leaned up and whispered in his ear, "I bet you didn't have guys like that in the publishing world." He nodded and laughed.

Ruben felt great walking home. Lightheaded from the drinks, he took in the excitement of the street—crowded bars, smiling couples, frantic music, and the smells of burgers and cigarettes. He was much older than the others on the street, but he felt like he was part of this world, even though he knew how silly it was to think that way. He might have most of his hair, his sharp features, and not many wrinkles; he might walk with a bounce; but he was an older guy. No doubt about it.

He spent the weekend planning. He had five classes—all freshmen. Ben had given him the curriculum and a plan to follow. Ruben had read all the stories and poems in the anthology and made up study plans for the first three weeks. He wanted to cover everything—leave nothing to chance.

Ruben lived alone, and had ever since his divorce. As an editor, he had done the serious work right here at his desk, where he would sit at a stool and hover over manuscripts, carefully removing what was not needed and adding what was missing. His specialty was nonfiction. One of his projects, a book of magic, earned a national editing award.

If he needed company, he'd meet the other editors for lunch, go to a ballgame with old college friends, or play poker or drink beer with his neighbors. That had been enough of a social life—usually.

Then one day while he was finishing a gardening book, he felt his concentration slipping away and in its wake harsh memories of his failed marriage floated by: vicious arguments in bed, vacations cut short, meals in silence, the decision to stay childless, the long drive home alone from the airport, the frowning and smirking lawyers.

Lately, he had been playing around with the idea of teaching, and somehow these memories of Edna made the notion seem more desirable. If nothing else, he would not be so alone. The people at work understood. It made sense for an editor to become an English teacher. He had always been good at explaining difficult concepts. And, the company was downsizing anyway.

Classes started off well. He assigned stories to read, discussed them in class, and gave quizzes and tests. The kids cooperated. Perhaps they knew he was older and deserved respect. He hoped they responded to his quiet confidence. He was pleased and surprised at how well it had gone. He had feared that once in the classroom, things would be different, but he had nothing to fear.

Every day at lunch Ruben sat with the other English teachers at a long table in the back of the cafeteria. "How do you like this shitty food?" they all wanted to know. He said he liked it, and he did. He had no taste in food. Food was food. Sometimes he sat next to a man named Bernie, the sponsor of the school newspaper. They talked about basketball. Yes, Ruben did plan to go to the high school games. He could see getting into that.

Alice was always there, perched at the end of the table with a novel and a small salad. Every so often, she'd look up from the book to laugh at the jokes—dirty and otherwise. When it came time to make fun of the principal, a former football player from Dallas, she'd join right in with a Texas drawl, "Well, I guess us coachin' guys can tell you faggots what to teach. If you don't like it, join another team. Sheee-it!"

One day she asked Ruben about editing. He told her how much he had loved smoothing out a book. He told her that he had just lost interest and maybe that's why he was here. He didn't mention Edna. The bell rang and they kept on talking. That's when he found out they were both free the next period and that she stayed on in the cafeteria to grade papers. Pretty soon he stayed on.

At first he graded papers, but soon he found he could talk and she would listen and smile and keep right on grading papers. He described how well his classes were going. Just like he'd imagined. "I ask them to read stories like 'To

Build a Fire,' and they read them. We talk about them. Then they write about them. And I read what they write and return it the next day."

"Well, you're an editor." She looked over and squinted at him. "You are what you do."

"It's what I did. I can show them what they need to do to write a more complete paper. I correct their grammar. I try to be positive. It works." She started to say something but then went back to her stack of AP essays.

That's how it usually went. He'd talk about his classes, she'd nod and smile, and then they would go back to work. Once she showed him what she was doing with her AP essays. He was impressed. "Serious stuff. I'm not ready for that yet."

All through the fall he would be there with her. Classes in the morning, lunch with the teachers, cafeteria with Alice, and a few more classes. When he passed an English teacher in the hall, he'd grin and make sure to say "SWARM" and offer a high five. It was okay. When he had decided to make this career change, he had no idea how quickly he would fit in.

They weren't always alone in the cafeteria. Jesse, one of the janitors, often stopped by. He was at the school when

Alice started twenty years ago. He'd stand by the window, smoke a cigar, and complain about the kids ("animals"), the teachers ("losers"), and the administrators ("morons"). He was especially bitter that "that asshole Evans fired my brother." Alice would smile and nod and keep on grading. Clyde Jones from the biology department occasionally appeared. He was a nervous little man who never seemed to have a reason for being there. When she introduced Clyde the first time, she told Ruben that several years ago they had served together on an evaluation committee. Usually he would sit and shuffle through his papers and sneak peeks at Alice. He never said anything to Ruben. When he talked to Alice, he would ask if she'd "read the latest." Another time he handed her a folder. "Make any changes you want. Stick to one-syllable words." But he wasn't there often and that was fine with Ruben.

Ruben knew that people might wonder what was going on with him and Alice. He wondered if any used the ridiculous term "in a relationship" to describe them. They were both single. But, it wasn't like they were sneaking off to make love in a bus. Anyway, the idea of being the subject of gossip appealed to him. He had never, as far as he could tell, been the subject of gossip.

On weekends he'd read papers and watch football. One Saturday evening, three of his former colleagues from the publishing house paid him a surprise visit.

"How about a drink?"

"Why not? I could use the company."

This brought a big laugh because at work, company was the last thing he needed.

They went to O'Reilly's, where they bought him three beers. They told him how his replacement couldn't do shit as an editor. He told them that teaching was just what he hoped. He liked activity. He got along with the kids and the teachers. He did not mention Alice. On the way back, one of the guys threw an arm around Ruben's shoulder, "I was a real prick in high school. Drove my teachers bat-shit. Watch out for students like me."

Right before winter break, Alice asked Ruben if he was going to the faculty party. He thought so.

"I'm not much of a party person," she said, "but this one is fun. All the teachers pack in to this local restaurant. Everyone is excited about heading out of town or at least being away for awhile."

"I know I'll enjoy it," he said.

She paused and then added, "I live a block away."

That day, for the first time, Ruben kicked a student out of class. The boy, one of the few scowlers, had come in late that day. He took a seat in the back, tipped back the desk, and started to whistle. The kids laughed. Ruben felt his throat tighten. He walked to the back and stood over the boy. "What's going on, Butch?" Butch smirked at him but said nothing. Ruben could feel the kids around him. He knew they were pulling for him. "Butch, when I'm teaching a class, I want you to listen. If you don't want to listen, go see the principal." With that, the boy stood up, shrugged, and staggered out the door.

When Ruben returned to the front of the room, he looked for the single sheet of paper with the day's lesson. He checked his briefcase. "Must have left it at home," he said to no one in particular. "Today," he announced to the class, "I'd like you to write a description of what you hope to be doing ten years from now. Where will you live? With whom? Where will you work? How about your hobbies?" Before long they were writing away, and he was able to relax and forget about Butch.

That night Ruben wondered if he was falling in love. Why else would he think so much about Alice? He'd lie awake remembering what she wore that day. He'd write her name on a pad and erase it. Silly stuff. Did she love him too? Yes, he believed she did. She knew who he was and how he got that way.

The party was good. A faculty band played old favorites. A retired history teacher, back from a trip to Africa, rattled off a long, drunken toast. Ruben and Ben high-fived after Ruben went through every letter of "SWARM." Ruben talked to the principal, who sounded just like Alice's impersonation of him. Earlier that week he had sent a memo to Ben urging him to require his teachers to "do more grammer." Ben, unable to resist the temptation, had stuck the note on the department bulletin board. Ruben and Alice danced. She was surprised he was so agile. And so was he. By leaving time, they were both a little drunk. Would he come back to her apartment for a drink? Why not? They walked down the sidewalk holding hands.

It was a teacher's apartment. Simple and organized. Novels and books of poetry. Prints and posters. Pictures of a farm. "My father grew up there," she said. "And then he moved to the small town where I grew up. But we used to visit the farm. It was in Iowa. Are you a farm boy, Ruben?"

"Oh, no. Pittsburgh." All this time together and they had never bothered to find out where the other grew up.

He sat on the couch, and she brought him a glass of white wine and sat in a chair across from him. She had poured herself a glass of something brown. The room was illuminated by an old lamp in the corner and from the light in the kitchen. Neither said anything.

Finally she spoke. "Together at last!" she blurted out, trying hard to be funny. There was another pause, and then she returned to her teacher voice. "You know, Ruben, I didn't like the idea of hiring an older person. I thought the school was trying to be trendy. I'm on record as being opposed to this experiment." She sipped her drink and looked away.

Ruben smiled, "No room for geezers." He felt pleased with his quick response.

"No room for geezers." She tucked a little humor back into her voice. "I don't have room in my life for anything else."

"I agree. You seem to pack your life well."

She stretched out her legs. "But then Old Ruben arrived unexpectedly."

"And…?"

"And I realized I have more room in my life than I thought." She was trying to sound matter-of-fact, but her voice quavered. This wasn't easy for her.

Ruben suddenly missed the rich silence of the cafeteria. He sat and looked and nodded but said nothing. She continued, "Am I making sense?"

"You are." And now he opened up a little. "You make me feel comfortable. Before, I always worked alone. I like working with someone else. I like the company of someone smart like you." He paused to say more but no words arrived. He threw out his hands helplessly.

Alice nodded and abruptly turned on the Texas accent, the one she used to ridicule the principal. "Pardner, we ain't talking so good." She stood up. "I'll be right back. These here dress-up clothes are gettin' to me." She patted him on the head and hurried down the hall.

He sat there thinking how much his life had changed, how one little choice had brought him into another world, how unsatisfied he would be if he were still back at the company struggling with someone else's work.

Across from him was a mirror. When he looked into it, he could see down the hall all the way to her room. It was a long hall for a little apartment. There were pictures hanging. Would he walk down the hall to her bedroom? Would he check out the pictures when he walked back?

The door opened and there was Alice. She had changed clothes, but instead of something revealing, she now wore sweatpants and the dangling modifier T-shirt from the fall party. But that was okay with him; actually, he liked this outfit better.

As she moved down the hall, he could see she was carrying a box, and even though she was far down the hall and even though the hall was long and dark, he, the former editor, recognized the contents immediately—a book manuscript. And it looked large.

Air
and Space

She opened the door to her hotel room right away and greeted him with a half hug. "How'd you sleep, Big Guy?"

"Not bad," he muttered.

"We can go downstairs and eat in the coffee shop. It has private booths." She moved past him down the hall, leaving in her wake a strong smell of perfume and tobacco. The hall had a thick maroon carpet; the walls were a faint blue and were covered with maps and pictures of past presidents and other Washington, D.C., history. She walked quickly, running her hands along the wall, touching the pictures but ignoring them. Greg hurried to keep up.

That's how she had walked yesterday—quickly and with a purpose. Gabbing about the displays in the museums, but not really paying attention. And she looked like she'd been working out. Used to be chubby. Not anymore. If Greg's dad had been here, he might have mumbled something about keeping fit to hump. And she might have said, "Thanks for the compliment," or she might have laughed in his face. You could never tell with her.

On the elevator, she smiled at him and pinched his cheek. They were about the same height; her hair was blonder, probably dyed. She reached out and touched his curly brown hair. "That was fun yesterday, Greg. I haven't played tourist for a long time. I'm glad your father had this idea."

"It was your idea. Dad wasn't so sure. Remember?"

"Well, it was a good idea. Gives mom and son a chance to be together. Maybe the wholesome experience of touring Washington will turn the little guy back into a model student. Let him go back to Forest High motivated."

"Hey, Mom, fuck off."

The elevator door opened up to a lobby full of people and luggage. Upscale, busy, people

The booth at the coffee shop was by the window facing M Street. Lots of dark people with funny hats hurrying by. Greg had never seen a place like Washington. When his eighth grade class had taken a trip here, he hadn't been allowed to go. Instead of flying to Washington, riding buses all over the place, and meeting his congressman, he slouched in the corner of Principal Spangler's office and stared at a grammar book and anyone who came in.

They both ordered scrambled eggs, sausage, potatoes, and buttered toast. "What was your favorite part of yesterday?" she asked.

"Air and Space Museum," he answered quickly as he took a bite of eggs.

She nodded and smiled.

"Why are you smiling?" He raised his voice.

"Don't all you guys like planes and other manly things?"

Her tone annoyed him. "I don't like what most 'guys' like, but I did like this. Okay?"

"Easy, Big Fella, I'll stop smiling. What about dinner?

Didn't you like the big steak? No doggie bag for the Gregster."

"It was okay."

Actually, he liked the steak a lot. His dad didn't take him out much and when he did, it was for pizza or tacos. Or maybe the Sizzler. His dad didn't like eating much. A twenty-five-dollar steak would have ruined his appetite.

While Greg had polished off his dinner his mother teased the waiter and joked with some boozy salesmen at the next table. This is what drove his dad crazy. She was a toucher. A stand-too-close girl. A flirt, plain and simple. Here she was, at it again. But Greg wasn't annoyed or disappointed because he had always known his mom liked to flirt, and he wasn't surprised that night three years ago when the screaming started. "Did it have to be a neighbor? Couldn't you have screwed someone from across town?" Greg could still hear the nasty laughter and then the slamming door. Just like in the movies.

That was three years ago. Now they were eating eggs together.

"So, my dear son, let's talk about it, okay?" She finished her breakfast and took a sip of her black coffee.

"It?"

"You. What you've been doing to make the school people call special meetings."

"You're not serious, are you? You want me to explain why I'm being such an asshole?"

"No one calls you that. They want to know why you've given up. Three years ago you were Mr. Sixth Grade. A real study nerd. Now, from what I've heard, you don't do much of anything, and, when you do, you don't do it very well or you cheat. So what's going on?"

He shrugged.

"Don't shrug."

"I'll shrug if I want, and stop pretending to be a parent."

"Fine, I'm just some outsider asking you why you've shut down."

"I don't know. And if I did know, it wouldn't matter."

He knew that everyone figured it was because of the divorce. When his dad kicked his mom out of the house, he turned a little quiet. He was never a real loudmouth, but the school was all over him with counselors. And somehow that pissed him off, so he turned silent and they sent in more people and then he decided he had to stay sullen. He didn't want all these silly people to think they knew what they were doing.

And then he felt guilty for acting this way around his dad, but he was mad at him for what he had done and he resented all the pathetic attempts his dad made to be buddies.

It was just easier to be mean.

"Well," his mom said as she waved to the waiter for a check, "maybe we'll talk about it on the plane." She reached for a cigarette and then remembered she couldn't smoke.

This past fall there had been a meeting with teachers, administrators, counselors, and his dad to talk about "the terrible attitude" Greg had brought with him to Forest High. Someone had asked about a mother. "Gone. Out of the picture. I'm a single parent," his dad had said ruefully. At that meeting people kept repeating what a fine student Greg had once been. He'd nod and then someone else would say the same thing. They wanted to make sure his dad knew what was going on. But he did know. Greg was silent at home, too.

Then, a month later, at a smaller and even more serious staffing, who should march in but the person who had helped raise him for the first twelve years of his life. She gave Greg a little kiss on the top of his head and sat down across from his father. "Hi, Hank."

"Hi, Dolores."

"Thanks for including me."

"We've tried everything else."

Everyone looked Greg's way, but he just kept staring at his knuckles. He was surprised to see his mom, but not amazed. He figured one day she would come back for a while. He didn't feel anything. Maybe later he would.

After introductions, the head counselor took over and repeated what Greg had been hearing all year. "We want Greg to complete this first year of high school with the right attitude. Right now, Greg, you have a bad attitude. You're a smart guy. You know how important school is. You used to be the smartest kid in class. But now you've just quit, and we'd like to help you."

The words were true. How could he argue with them? But he just sat there, just as he did when his dad tried to motivate him. The longer he did nothing, the harder it was to do anything. That would mean adults were right, and he refused to give them credit for anything. It was easier to sit there. It was easier not to imagine what his life would be like if he continued like this.

"Punishment hasn't worked," his mom interrupted. "I've got an idea. I'll take him to Washington, D.C., for a long weekend. This will make up for missing the trip last year, Greg, and maybe we can talk."

His father shrugged. The school people said why not. Greg just sat there, but he didn't object.

And now here they were at a coffee shop after spending the day before at museums and monuments.

"I've got to go back up to the room for a little while," his mom said after paying. "Meet you in the lobby and then we're off to the Hirshhorn Museum." She hurried away.

In the lobby, he looked at the *Washington Post* and then at all the people. It was so strange to be sitting somewhere and no one paid the least bit of attention to him. If he smirked or yawned now, no one would notice. No more audience. Did these people wonder why he was out of school? He took a look at a brochure for something at the National Geographic Museum. His dad did take him to museums, but he tried too hard, and he'd lose his temper if Greg didn't act interested. Then they'd break it off and go home. The silence in the car driving back would be unbearable.

With his mom, at least there wasn't the awful silence.

On the plane to D.C., she told him that her old boyfriend, the neighbor, turned out to be "a first-class prick." She dumped him and went back home to Madison, found a job at the hospital, and made lots of new friends. Greg had fallen asleep on the plane listening to her describe each new friend.

Now in the lobby, he was starting to wonder about his mom when the elevator doors opened and out she came, all smiles. "Cab time, Big Boy. More museums." He followed her out the door. In the cab, she chattered on about a call she got from a roommate who was about to move in with her boyfriend. She said that a man on the elevator, "a big black guy with a turban," was trying to look down her blouse.

As they pulled up in front of the museum, Greg spoke up. "Are you going to marry again, Mom?"

"You're kidding, aren't you?" She handed the cabbie some money. "Keep the change, honey."

At the Hirshhorn his favorite was the WPA art exhibition. He studied a painting of a minor league ballpark at night. His dad had played minor league ball. He was a good athlete. He'd like to coach. The painting was realistic but not really: the players were all stretched out and the crowd was all blended together. But it was baseball and it was at night and it made Greg feel good.

He looked to his right. His mom was talking to a younger man in a green sweater, bow tie, and brown pants. She was standing close and doing her usual touching. Bow tie was beaming. She touched him on the shoulder, and he leaned over and whispered and then was off down the hall.

She joined Greg at the baseball painting. "Very colorful, but I never understood why people like this sport. Too bad the artist didn't have a camera. Let's go back to the hotel. I could use a nap."

In the cab, she asked about dinner. "Should we eat at the hotel or that Italian place across the street?"

"Do you care?" Greg yawned.

"Not really." She was holding an unlit cigarette in her hand. Her forehead was touching the window.

"Then I'll just have room service."

"You sure?" She kept looking out the window and fiddling with the cigarette.

"I'm sure. Then I'll watch a movie."

"Getting tired of your old lady?" She faked a little girl whine.

"No, I just want to be by myself."

"Then come by in the morning. Just like today—for breakfast." The cab pulled up in front of the hotel. She paid the driver and then walked up to the uniformed doorman and asked him for a light. Greg walked through the crowded lobby to the elevator.

At 2 A.M., Greg's phone rang. It was his mom. "Greg, honey, I met some people and went to a party. I'm going to sleep in, so let's skip breakfast." He could hear music and shouting in the background.

"Did you meet the guy you were talking to at the museum? The bow-tie guy?"

"Smart fellow you are." She slurred the words.

"I've been to Washington with my mother, remember."

"How was the room service?"

"Burger and fries and a milkshake. The burger was cold."

"And the movie? Hope you didn't get some hard-core porn. Your dad wouldn't like that."

"I took a long walk and then came back and slept. Or I slept until some lady called me at 2 A.M."

"A walk? At night? Do you do that often?"

"Never have before."

"Interesting... Anyway, let's meet in the lobby at noon."

She spoke in a low, halting voice. "Tomorrow, we can go to the White House and maybe back to Air and Space. And then back to Chicago."

There was a long pause, and then she continued, "We'll talk seriously on the plane. We all think you're just too young to quit."

Funny in
the Summer

Armand looked up from his book as a rangy blond girl with a red headband strode into the empty teachers' cafeteria. She swept past the table where, during the year, bridge players hung out, and came right up to where he was sitting by himself at a corner table. "I'm Julie Perkins," she held out her hand. "The new English teacher slash assistant basketball coach. I sat right behind you at the meeting this morning. And you're?"

Armand looked up, shook her hand, and mumbled his name. He remembered the young person at the summer school faculty meeting.

She sat down across from him, pulled a water bottle from her bag, and kept right on talking. "What's it like teaching summer school?"

Armand blinked and sat up straight. "Don't ask me. I've never taught summer school before. I suppose the place will feel empty. When I'm here during the year, it's crawling with kids." He thought about the halls of Forest High School clogged with jabbering young people. He kept his voice neutral. No reason to be rude, but he felt no interest in bantering.

"Never been here in the summer!" *Or any other time,* Armand thought. Julie reached over and patted his hand. "Home alone!" she laughed. "You can hang out in the auto shop or practice kicking field goals outside."

Armand smiled but not much. "Or I could put on one-man plays in the drama department or snooze in one of the buses or I could take the bus for a spin." He paused.

"Actually, I wouldn't be here this summer at all except that Jimmy Sanders inherited a cleaning business and moved back to Peoria. I'm doing the English department a favor." Even though he found himself talking, Armand was still not used to people coming over to his table, much less touching him. During the year, with bridge players and other faculty people filling the tables, he might have politely let this newcomer know he didn't want company.

For decades he had graded papers at this table by himself. He had plenty of time to be with others at faculty parties and on the golf course, but in the cafeteria he never did much talking.

"Well then, it must really feel different?" the girl continued. "It's got to feel creepy with the building so empty. Kind of odd." Julie was chewing gum, and she raised her eyebrows when she spoke and looked right into his eyes.

"Little things will be odd, I guess," Armand said. "Like teaching in shorts. I'm not sure what the kids will have to say about my knees. But I guess they should see them before I retire."

She stopped chewing her gum and stared at him. "You're not thinking of packing it in, are you?"

"Not for a few years. But I am in my sixties." He couldn't

believe he was having this conversation with a stranger.

"And then what? An old folks' reservation?"

He shook his head and told her he planned to read and to garden. He had an offer from a local publisher to work on a textbook project. In the summer he'd play golf. In the winter he'd travel. Plus he could do some consulting for the school district. "Actually, I'm looking forward to my retirement. I know how to fill up my time."

"That sounds great, Armand." Now she was calling him by his first name. "Just be sure you do it. Don't quit. We had a neighbor in Ohio who sat so long in front of the TV set after he retired that he had to have his legs amputated. Can you imagine that? They chopped off his legs because he didn't use them. You don't ever want to quit."

It was dumbfounding that this person could talk so matter-of-factly about quitting. Did she know that only two weeks ago he had been named Forest's "Teacher of the Decade"? At the end-of-the-year party, the superintendent had presented Armand with a plaque and then proclaimed, "Most of us start shrinking, but this guy keeps growing." Not one teacher who watched him tearfully accept the award would ever think of him as a quitter.

Armand cleared his throat and looked around the empty

room. During the school year the cafeteria smelled like soup and hot dogs. Now it smelled more like wax. The sound of the milk machine from across the room reached his ears. He turned back and noticed how athletic Julie looked—short, blond hair, boyish face, erect posture, and the gum. When the assistant principal introduced her at the morning meeting, he said that she had coached JV basketball at Lehigh.

"What are you doing at Forest?" Armand suddenly asked. Was he being polite? Curious? He wasn't sure.

She tipped her chair back and started to talk. Thirteen years before, she had been about to start teaching, but then Bud came along and she married him. "He knew all about software—how to make it, use it, and improve it. Bill Gates wanted to hire him. Bud wanted me to have time for business trips, so I turned down my first teaching job. He was so serious and alert that I couldn't resist him. A very serious guy."

They traveled to Abu Dhabi, Bangladesh, Bolivia, Andorra, Manchuria, and Bhutan. They even spent a month in Albania. They traveled so much that they never had a family or a place to live. Then one day outside of an inn in the Cotswolds, she found Bud slumped over the steering wheel of their rented Land Rover. A massive heart attack. "I loved him, Armand, but he was exhausting. Too smart. Too much energy. It was horrible to see a guy with so much future sprawled out dead." *Sprawled out?* Armand wondered if she had carried him from the car before she called the British police.

Fifteen minutes into this conversation and she had told him all of this. A few minutes later she started in on him. "Are you married?"

"Not anymore. I was married once to a vice president of a downtown bank." He paused. He could hear the drone of the floor-waxing machine. The sound carried in the empty building. "We didn't like each other." That was all he needed to tell her.

"Did splitting up make you sad?" Julie reached down to retie her jogging shoes. She was still chewing gum. But she kept her eyes on him.

"Not really. It was going to happen." Actually he had been relieved to tear loose from Audrey, who had come to consider him a total loser. Sometimes at night, when he was grading papers, he would hear fierce breathing behind him. He would turn and find a scowling Audrey shaking her head. She would usually mutter something and stalk back to watch TV in the bedroom. Audrey had no idea how much he loved writing his precise, helpful comments on student themes. She could not imagine how good it felt to return them promptly. This was how it had to be done. Then one night, Audrey poured a pot of black coffee into his briefcase, drenching a batch of senior term papers. The next day they both called lawyers. Instead of telling Julie all of this, he simply added, "It was a good thing, a very good thing for both of us." After Audrey, he had dated an American History teacher. They had gone to plays and movies together. Occasionally she'd spend the night. She was retired now in North Carolina, and Armand figured maybe he'd see her from time to time after he retired.

Julie changed the subject. "What are you teaching this summer?"

He told her he planned for his students to write several long personal narratives and to read *Catcher in the Rye, The Great Gatsby, Billy Budd,* and other novels. "It's American Literature, and I can do pretty much what I want."

"Are you as good an English teacher as they say?" She stared hard at him.

"They?"

"The other teachers and the principal."

"Yes. I am." He leaned over and grabbed his old leather briefcase but remained sitting. "I've got to meet a friend for dinner."

"I'm going to play softball. See you tomorrow, Armand. Your room is next to mine." He thought about walking out with her, but instead he stayed seated and watched her march through the room and out the door. "See ya," she called back.

The next day classes started, and Armand arrived early at his windowless classroom, which was used during the regular year by coaches who taught health and driver's education. The walls were bare except for a poster of Peyton Manning, whose teeth had been turned into Dracula fangs. On the door was a poster of an AIDS victim—an emaciated black child with bulging eyes. The caption read, "Condom Sense." On the wall was also an old photo of Forest High. It had been taken early in the century. Armand was studying it when the door opened and in walked Julie in blue shorts and an orange Hawaiian shirt. "You know, Armand," she laughed, pointing at his shorts, "you might be right about those knees."

Now that they were both standing, he could see that

Julie was a little taller than he was, but not much. "Back to teacher pants tomorrow?" he asked.

"Might be a good idea. It's all about dignity."

"No gum today?"

"Not with the kids."

He cleared his throat. "Ready to teach?" It was the right thing to say, but he was curious to see how far her confidence went.

"I'm ready, Coach. I'm ready to get some freshmen prepared for the rigors of English. They'll write about what they 'know' and what they 'should know.' They'll read short stories and take a few trips." With that she held up a fist, waited until he hand-bumped her, and left to teach.

After class she joined him in the cafeteria. "I'm going to like it here," she smiled. "One of my kids wrote about his uncle's tattoo parlor."

"Any discipline problems?"

"Nope. After all, I am a coach, and I've been around the world," she laughed. "These are just little suburban geeks. And anyway the summer makes them mellow."

Armand told her about his first class. "We read a Poe story and talked about it. Before that, we talked about what goes into a good story. Then we shared some stories."

"Any good ones?"

"A girl named Cindy described waking up her grandmother. She didn't know that old lady kept her false teeth in a glass next to her bed. Cindy screamed and ran out of the room."

"Did you laugh?"

"We all laughed."

"Armand," Julie lowered her voice, "you are a funny guy. You look like a regular old school teacher with your gray hair and glasses, but I think you are really a funny guy. Am I right?"

Her question surprised him and made him feel a little uncomfortable. "You're wrong." He raised his voice more than he needed to. "I know when to laugh, but I am definitely not funny. And I'm certainly not a 'funny guy.'" He shook his head back and forth for several seconds.

"Well, you remind me of a lot of funny people I know. Don't the kids laugh in your classes?" She pulled her chair up to the table and leaned her head on her hand.

"Sure, but I'm not funny." He meant it.

"But I bet you know what's funny. I bet things amuse you. What's the funniest thing that happened last year in school?" She was not going to stop.

What an odd question! But instead of telling her that he had to grade his papers, he just started talking. "Last fall in the middle of a class, out of the blue, a student raised her hand and said she thought it was great that we had a holiday honoring the doctors who took care of animals. She thought Veterans Day was Veterinarians Day."

"Veterinarians Day!" Julie said. "Did you all laugh? I would have laughed."

"I tried not to, but after a while I cracked up. The class went crazy, of course. And Franny laughed, too. But I felt sorry for her, so we talked after class." In fact Armand was not sure that Franny understood her mistake. When he explained that a veteran was someone who had been in a war, she just shrugged.

Julie took a drink from her bottle. "Nice job. You didn't want to hurt her. I told you that you were funny." For a second Armand was afraid she was going to pinch his chin, but she just leaned back and smiled and asked for another story.

Within seconds he was describing a student production of *A Christmas Carol*. "It was directed by a first-year teacher who didn't know what he was doing, and it was a disaster. Near the end, Marley's ghost got his chain caught in the hot-air register. When he tugged, it stayed stuck and dust came up. People in the front row thought the auditorium was on fire."

Julie laughed hard. "Good stuff, Armand. I can see some pimply kid tugging at the chain while all the grandmothers in the audience sprint for the exits."

"That's pretty much what happened." He was pleased with her reaction.

"It must be great to have all that stuff in your head."

"Don't worry. When you're my age, you'll have plenty."

"I hope so. I hope what's in there will be funny." She paused and stared down at the table. "Got to go. I have a softball game at 5:50, and then I've got to grade papers." She lowered her voice into mock seriousness, "We'll continue this tomorrow." She patted him on the shoulder and hurried off.

Every afternoon they met after class in the empty cafeteria. She told him what she had done that day—always well planned, always well executed. He'd describe his class —lots of writing and discussion. Then they would leave together. They would usually stop at the 7-Eleven where he bought a large coffee. Then they walked to her apartment and sat on the porch swing where he told her funny stories. He told her about bringing the wrong tests to a final, about a freshman who sailed a desk out the window, about a student who threw up in the reserve room of the library, about a teacher who had been locked in the bathroom all night long.

She loved his stories, and he knew why. *How much easier with you than Bud,* she must be thinking. *You're not an intense, young genius with sharp edges. You're well worn. Sure, you're getting bald, and you have a paunch, but so what? I like your world. I can see it.* She might even have boyfriends who played softball with her and maybe drank beer and spent the night. But none of them could give her what Armand could. That's why she hung around him. And, of course, the school was empty. Who else could she talk to?

Sometimes they sat on the school lawn together. It was there that he told her about the sophomore who had once conducted an experiment by crossing out the *c* in "cold milk" to make it read "old milk." The student claimed a significant drop in milk sales. The same afternoon on the lawn, Armand recalled a time when one of his colleagues —to give his students real-life experience—invited them to steal everything in the building and bring it back to the class. They did. He almost lost his job.

Sometimes they would talk about her sports life, but almost always they came back to his stories. One of her favorites concerned a girl in a creative writing class. All semester long the girl had refused to turn in stories, promising to give him a "complete work" in June. And she did: five stories copied from *Winesburg, Ohio.* Armand was astonished she had plagiarized so brazenly and a little hurt that she thought he wouldn't recognize such a well-known work. "I love it," Julie crowed. "I can't wait for my first plagiarist."

He remembered people he hadn't thought of in years. There was little Teddy Whitman, the introverted biology teacher from Butte, Montana. At faculty meetings, Teddy would nudge the man sitting next to him and nod in the direction of a female teacher. "See her?" he'd whisper. "I'd like to process her data." Or, "I'd like to lubricate her chassis," or "I'd like to tune her piano," or "I'd like to snake out her pipes." This continued until Teddy retired.

"What would Teddy say about me?" Julie asked. "Would he want to lubricate my chassis?" She was grinning.

"No comment." Armand felt uncomfortable.

"Don't look so embarrassed, Armand. Teddy would have noticed me, though. Wouldn't he?"

"Oh, yes. He would have noticed you." He paused and swallowed. No other words could come out.

"Okay," she laughed. "Tell me another story about a field trip."

And always she listened. "How could that happen?" she might ask. "Tell me that story again. I love it." And finally she would laugh—a long, sincere, lovely laugh, a laugh that told him how happy she was to be with him. And when she finally stopped laughing, she would keep on smiling.

The night before summer school ended, Armand sat in his study and made a long list of teaching memories. He started with the letter *A*. *A* could be Antonio, who used to sing in class, or *A* could be *All Quiet on the Western Front,* or the apricot someone stuck in his briefcase. For each letter, he jotted down memories until he had filled several pages. He was appalled at how much of himself he could pour out so quickly.

But then he thought about Julie. He could picture her rocking back and forth on the squeaky porch swing, eagerly prodding him to keep telling stores. Behind her was a lush green lawn and flowers. The smell of summer was everywhere. Soon he would have to imagine her somewhere else. But where? Where would she be? In the summer, they could leave together, and no one was there to notice. In the fall everyone would notice. Would she still come to his table? Would they sit next to each other at assemblies? Would she still want to hear funny stories? Would he have any to tell?

The next morning he taught his last class and then met Julie in the cafeteria. Before they said anything, a grinning man burst into the cafeteria and headed their way.

"Who's that?" Julie asked. The man had a gray beard, a green backpack, and a deep tan.

"Bob Hastings, another English teacher."

"Why the glum voice?"

"I didn't sleep last night."

Bob hurried over to them. "Armand, my boy! Who's the lady?" He pulled out a chair, turned it around, and straddled it. Armand introduced Julie.

"Here I go off fishing and hiking for the summer with my girlfriend, and the place falls apart." He pounded with mock anger on the table. "Do you realize, my dear, that no one sits at Armand's table?"

"It's summer. Different rules, I guess. I enjoy hearing his funny stories." Her voice was scarcely inflected.

"Armand 'funny'? I suppose so. What have you been doing, Old Boy, watching *Comedy Central?* Does he tell you jokes after school too?" Hastings stretched out his arms.

"All the time—usually over at my place." Her voice flattened even more as she stared back at Hastings, who reached over and poked Armand in the neck. "Armand, you old devil, whatever have you been doing?"

Armand stared at his hands. "I'm funny in the summer, I suppose. Who would have guessed?"

"Honey," Hastings stood up and looked down at Julie, "one thing we all know is that this funny guy sitting next to you is the real thing. No one works harder. No one is better prepared." Then, as he started to edge away, "I'm back to pick up a few class lists, and that's it until September. So long, you two."

They walked home slowly and ended up on her swing. The humid weather made Armand feel especially tired.

"You look different," Julie announced after they sat down.

"I'm tired, Julie. And I don't really like this heat." The swing felt uncomfortable against his back. The wood scratched his bare legs.

"You're slouching. And your voice sounds kind of trembly."

"That's my old man's voice. Maybe I should get a pony-tail to counteract it." He didn't feel like talking.

"It's not important." She shrugged and reached into her pocket for a stick of gum.

"Hastings is quite a guy," Armand said softly. "He can be very entertaining. Lots of energy."

"Hastings," she stopped chewing her gum, "is an asshole."

Armand ignored her. "Now there's someone with really funny stories. You'll find out next year." His words felt tight and stupid.

"Oh, please, Armand, please. The only thing I like about that phony is he gives me the courage to say what we've both been thinking for a long time."

"What's that?" Armand's stomach felt jumpy.

"Let's go inside," Julie said softly. "School's over for the summer. We've got other things to take care of, and you know it."

Armand heard himself breathe. His arms, already perspiring, felt even wetter. Had he ever felt more awkward?

"Julie," he stammered, "I have never thought about going to bed with you. I really haven't."

"Never? You have never thought about making love with me? You've never thought about us together?"

"Never in a serious way. I'm chasing retirement. You're

just getting started. Believe me. You have made me funny; making love would not be funny."

"You'll do just fine." She put her hand on his knee. She didn't wear a ring or nail polish.

"I just can't." He moved her hand away. "Julie, I can't. I'm a funny guy remember? Not a sexy one."

"Can't you be both?"

"Obviously not."

She took the gum out of her mouth, balled it up, and tossed it on the lawn. He looked across the street. On the far sidewalk a man was reading a book while walking his dog. When he looked back she was on her feet and shaking her hands at her sides, as if she was loosening up for a marathon. Her eyes were glistening. "Coaches don't cry," she sniffed. "Coaches shouldn't cry."

"English teachers do all the time." He stood up awkwardly and put his hands behind his head. "I think I'll go to Wisconsin for the rest of the summer." He often rented a small place near Green Bay. Then he hugged her. She was solid, of course, but she also felt soft and for one second he thought about walking with her inside. But instead he pulled away his arm and walked across the lawn to the sidewalk and turned toward his apartment.

He stopped at Kelly's Tap for three scotches. Tim, the security guard, and a few of his buddies shouted to him from a table in the rear. Back home, he turned on the ball game and watched the Cubs lose in extra innings.

Armand parked his Toyota in the front lot, which had been closed all summer long. He noticed that the "You Are Entering Cougar Country" sign had been given a fresh coat of paint. For the first time since June he entered Forest High School through the front door. Inside he saw that the lockers had been repainted a bright red to match the school's colors. The trophy case along the far wall featured the trophy won by the girls' soccer team for placing third in the state last spring. A "Welcome Class of 2013" banner hung over the doorway into the main classroom building. The floor, ferociously polished by Rocco and his crew, glistened like an ice rink. Without the hordes of teenagers, Forest High School smelled fresh and airy—but with a whiff of forbidden cigarette smoke.

"Hey, Mr. Waterman." It was Tim, the security guard. He was sitting on the bench with a *Weekly World News* in his lap. The headline read "Girl Born with Monkey Head." Tim was wearing a T-shirt with a faded picture of Bart

Simpson skateboarding. He looked up and smiled at Armand. "Welcome back. How's the most respected teacher in the school?" He cupped a cigarette in his thick hand.

"I'm okay, Tim. But we saw a lot of each other this summer. You don't need to welcome me back." Tim had been Armand's student back in 1970, his first year as a teacher at Forest. Most of his class had gone on to college. Tim went to Vietnam. When he returned home, he tried to become a police officer but failed the exam three times. Then D.F. "Porky" Boyd, the longtime Forest High School security guard, dropped dead while breaking up a fight after a basketball game. Superintendent Hayes believed in helping local kids—especially veterans—and he hired Tim to replace the "Venerable Boyd."

"I didn't forget about the summer." Tim coughed and pounded his chest. "I just like saying 'welcome back.' This was your first summer school ever wasn't it?" Tim knew things like that. He might be a bit thick, but he knew who taught where and when and sometimes even how.

"First and last." Armand paused and swallowed. "I had an interesting time, but summer should be spent on the golf course or at Wrigley Field. I was glad to help out, but no more."

"I hear we have a new English teacher." To cover his smile, Tim brought the cigarette to his mouth. He had pink, chapped skin and a belly that hung over his sweatpants. *In a few days,* Armand thought, *he will be wearing his uniform, which will make him appear more streamlined.*

"I don't know much about that, Tim." Armand hurried off down the hall. He half expected one more remark from Tim. He was certain that at this moment, his former student's chubby face had dropped into a gaping grin.

Rocco knew just how to set up his room. The desks were arranged in a semicircle the way Armand liked them. The empty bulletin board was ready for his things. The flowers and plants along the windowsill were back and blooming. Those Italian janitors really knew how to keep things alive. From the closet he pulled out a box labeled "September." In it were posters of individual writers—Thoreau, Poe, Toni Morrison, Maya Angelou. Another poster had several smaller photos of Joyce, Synge, Yeats, Shaw, and other Irish writers. He knew where on the empty walls to tack each of these. In another part of the closet he found a large calendar, which he hung next to the bulletin board. The bulletin board itself would be used for announcements of movies, plays, and readings. It would also be the place for cartoons.

He pulled open the drawer of his desk. Inside were Cuban cigars Rocco had left for him. Instead of the cigars, he pulled out his lesson book for the year and opened it to page one. Once again he would plan the entire year from memory. In no time at all, it would all be written down—the classes, tests, papers, field trips. The old planning books were filed away just in case, but he never bothered to look at them. Any changes would be for the good. Normally, he never checked; this year he might have to. In the afternoon, he would study his class lists. Lately children of former students had been turning up in his classes. Later, he would meet Cummings for a steak. Cummings might fill him in on his summer travels. He was even closer to retirement than Armand.

On his way out of the school, Armand stopped in the office. He looked first at the general announcement board. Doreen Elders, a longtime Forest secretary, had died this summer. Colleagues were urged to send money to the lung cancer association. He wrote a short note thanking Rocco for the cigars and stuck it in Rocco's mailbox. In his own box was the agenda for the next day's meeting. And there was a letter from Greece. He walked out of the office, down the hall, and out the building. He stood on the front steps and opened the letter.

My Dear Armand,

I have taken a job in Athens. I think you'll agree this is a good idea.

Thanks for the summer, Funny Guy. I don't plan to forget you.

Love,

Julie

He hadn't figured she would leave the country. Of course, she would know people in all those foreign places. They would have schools and jobs for young teachers—especially ones who could coach.

He considered buying a cup of coffee and walking down Julie's street, but instead he sat down in the grass near a soccer goal and looked back at the school. In July the two of them had sat in the same spot, and he described Audrey pouring coffee into his briefcase. He told Julie how he pulled out the soaked papers one at a time and how he crouched in the bathtub drying each sheet with Audrey's blow-dryer.

They both laughed hard at that one, but now when he thought about the two of them laughing together, all he could do was wish that he was back in his classroom surrounded by hundreds and hundreds of ungraded papers.

"Isn't That Abbie Hoffman Over There?"

Most people, if they remember Abbie Hoffman at all, picture a bearded, wild-eyed revolutionary who nominated a pig for president at the 1968 Democratic Convention in Chicago and who, a year later, was a defendant in a hugely publicized political "conspiracy" trial also in Chicago. And where one day—I still have a picture of it—he walked into the courtroom on his hands. Abbie represented the sixties for lots of us. He was rude. He named his kid Amerika. He wrote a book called *Steal This Book.* He appeared on a TV talk show sporting an American flag shirt that was blurred out by the network.

Anyway, people like me, who started teaching in the '60s, know all about Abbie Hoffman and what he stood for. But I have another memory—a more personal one that involved the end of a promising friendship. And the reason I recall it so vividly now is that Tim, the person who should have been my friend, just died.

Back in 1968, I was attending an English teachers' conference in Chicago. On the second day, I was sitting in the back row of a session called "Keeping Our Sanity." The speaker was a former teacher and now a time-management guru who used graphs, charts, and clever anecdotes to tell teachers how to plan classes, instruct one hundred or more students, grade papers, and still have time to go fishing. The big word was "manage." I scribbled down a few of his ideas for a report for my department chair back at Forest High. Next to me was another young teacher also jotting down a few notes. When the session wound up, he looked over at me. "The guy meant well, but he's full of shit. But you can't put 'full of shit' in your notes." He looked down at the pad in my lap. "Or in my notes," he said, holding up his own scribbling. "Let's go downstairs for a drink. My name's Tim."

Downstairs was a bar called Trader Vic's, well known for its rum drinks. We talked a little about our schools, families, and hobbies. Tim, married for a year, taught at a small school downstate and liked to garden. I taught at Forest High, had a wife, and liked to play golf. But mostly we talked about all the crap we had to ignore as young teachers. We both were off to good starts, in part because we didn't question the crap. We played the game. Now here, with the help of a few rum punches, we could share some deeper thoughts about the administration, department chairmen, ungrateful students, and conniving parents— the folks who ruled our lives. We'd always begin our rants with, "I've never said this before, but...." Nothing that we said was interesting, but we meant it. We really did mean it.

The next year, we met again at the same conference. Just as we had done the year before, we drank and talked a little about our wives and families and a lot about our dull-witted principals, our deadbeat students, the pointless paperwork, the shitty school food, and all the money we would never make because we were teachers. It was good-hearted and harmless bitching, and hardly original. But we weren't colleagues, so we could be as honest as we wanted. And we could be specific and maybe even tell some lies.

Tim left to go to the men's room and call home, and I sat alone and started to imagine this scene repeating year after year after year. The two of us would grow gray and paunchy and forgetful, but we'd keep returning. Tim might come up to Chicago for a Cubs game, and my wife and I might visit him and take a drive to his parents' farm. But it was at this conference that we'd enjoy each other the most. And if this conference moved elsewhere, we'd go elsewhere just to keep this long-distance friendship alive.

I didn't say anything about this when Tim came back to our table. How could I say, "Let's be lifelong friends" to someone I was just getting to know? Still, I had a strong suspicion that he felt this way too. If not, he would feel this way soon.

After we finished griping about our schools, we ridiculed the speaker from the morning's conference. This guy, a pretentious, cliché-driven, red-faced curriculum coordinator from Iowa, had blathered on about "raising the bar." He was full of himself and silly. A real windbag. He wore a yellowish leisure suit. He had dandruff. Before long, Tim took off his glasses and did a half-decent impersonation of this guy—gestures and all.

He beamed. "If you liked that, you'll really like my version of our former football coach who is now our principal." He frowned, hunched his shoulders, pretended to spit, and tugged at his crotch. "Tim, your colickular concerns is first rate. But the room is not too neat. Bad example. Be firm and consistent." Tim went on and on in the husky voice of this man I had never met, finally stopping but looking thoroughly pleased with himself. "I could never do that in Mt. Vernon. Word would get back and they'd run me out of town and maybe beat the shit out of me."

I was getting ready to describe the principal at my school, a nice enough fellow but clueless when it came to helping a serious teacher improve. He, too, was a former coach. I wasn't going to act him out, but I had some good stories Tim would like. Again, I had the eerie confidence that this joking, boozy chatter with Tim was going to continue throughout our careers. This might seem odd, but you had to be there.

But just as I started to describe Principal Tomkins telling a bad joke at a gathering of teachers, Tim grabbed my arm and pointed at a table in the middle of the room and glanced back. "Chris, isn't that Abbie Hoffman over there?" He was pointing at a bearded guy drinking and laughing with a bunch of other people. This guy was obviously the center of attention. The others, not notable in any way, clearly enjoyed listening to this man.

But, as engaging as he might be, I was certain he was not Abbie. "You're wrong, Tim. He's too young and clean. And his buddies look more like young Republicans."

Tim wasn't sure and he wasn't that pleased with what I had said. "He's here in Chicago for the conspiracy trial. He looks just like him. He just might come to a teachers' conference. There are a lot of antiwar folks here."

I became more insistent, probably more than I needed to be. I pointed out that Abbie would not like a bunch of teachers and that he would not be found dead at a place where people drank rum drinks featuring tiny umbrellas. "He's more likely to be on the North Side at the No Exit Café. Or, he might be hanging out with the other defendants at the Earl of Old Town saloon." I half-smiled. It might have resembled a smirk. But inside I was angry. I wanted to keep drinking and talking to Tim. I wanted to tell him about the people at my school. I wanted to encourage him to do more impersonations. I wanted to talk baseball.

Tim was determined. "I'm going over there to talk him. I want to introduce myself."

He stood up.

Now even more people started looking at us. "Tim, don't. Please don't. You'll make a fool of yourself. Anyway, what can you do? Get his autograph? Stay here. Let's have another drink and keep swapping stories about our idiot administrators. Tomorrow we're leaving."

He ignored me. Tim was a little guy with reddish hair and a fair complexion. His face was all red. He was breathing hard. I reached up and grabbed his arm and held him there. He didn't fight me, and he stopped. Meanwhile, the bearded fellow and his people were standing up and moving toward the door.

Tim pulled free and dropped back in his chair. "I don't get it, Chris. Why did it matter if I made a fool of myself? Why does it matter to you or anyone else?" He was dead serious. He wasn't going to settle for a silly answer from me so we could return to our conversation.

I had no answer. Nothing I could say would explain why this mattered so much right now. I sat there and stared back stupidly at Tim, who was staring at me. Finally I shrugged and asked the waiter for the check. But when the waiter arrived back at the table, Tim told him we'd decided to stay. He ordered two more rum drinks and began apologizing to me. I was right about Abbie, he said. Abbie would not want to talk to some second-rate English teacher from some cow town in Illinois. He'd prefer a sophisticated fellow from a school like Forest High.

I ignored the sarcasm and watched as Tim gestured to two ladies who walked in carrying bags of English materials. "Ladies, join us for some booze." And then—unbelievably—the guy who looked like Abbie was back in the room, and he sat down with us.

And then things got crazier.

Tim handled the introductions. The ladies, Gert and Betty, were sisters from Rockford. They both taught high school English, mostly American lit. The man with the beard jokingly announced his name actually was Abbie. Obviously, he had overheard us. "Do you mean it?" I asked. And he replied with a grin, "You'll never know."

Tim, of course, was all over him with questions about the convention, the trial, and the protest movement. The bearded man answered with short and not very helpful answers and kept smiling wryly at something behind me. I turned and spotted his buddies across the room. They had moved to a different table and were taking in the whole thing.

I was furious. I nudged Tim and told him to look over at the far table. He ignored me and kept on talking to the ladies about Abbie's antics. Then he ordered more drinks for all of us.

I left some money on the table and staggered toward the door. I stopped and waved to the group in the corner. Then I gave them the finger. They waved back and laughed. One of the Rockford ladies called back from the table. She hoped to see me again. The other lady was listening to more of Tim's talk about the '68 Convention.

I went to the men's room and was joined at the urinal by the Abbie guy. We joked, but he could see I was mad and confused. In the hall we kept half-talking and then I pulled him toward me and talked right into his face. "I know just what you're doing. You're putting on a show for your buddies. You'll have something to talk about for years. You're a real prick."

And that's when he pushed me. I think he wanted to hit me, but this was easier and made the point. I sat down hard. He disappeared back into the bar area. I pulled myself back on my feet and followed him. He headed right for the table with his buddies. They left through another door and I just stood in the middle of the room in a drunken, embarrassed, confused stupor.

Ten minutes later, I was passed out on my bed.

The next day, Tim and I met in the hall in front of a room where a teacher from London was going to talk about developments in Great Britain. We had both intended to go, but instead we walked downstairs to the coffee shop. We sat in a corner booth and drank black coffee. I had some toast. Tim had a V8 and that was all.

We talked about our hangovers. Tim claimed his was the worst ever. "I don't drink like you guys." I wasn't sure what he meant by "you guys," but I didn't bother to ask him. It didn't make much sense since I am not much of a drinker.

Then I mentioned the bearded guy. Tim didn't say much, so I rambled. I was quite sure—positive, actually— that he wasn't the real Abbie Hoffman. He didn't really look like him.

Tim just stared at his juice, and I went on. I said that it just didn't make sense for anyone to do what he did—

pretend to be Abbie and actually perform for his friends. It didn't make sense. Maybe he liked being a character. Maybe this happened a lot and he had developed this routine. He might have been drunk, and we all know what drink does.

"Chris," Tim suddenly spoke up, "you sound just like an English teacher. Don't we always ask our students to explain why some character did such and such? Don't we do that? And—God forbid—if a character's action is not motivated, we're all over the author. Well, I'm not going to treat this bearded phony like Hamlet or Holden Caulfield. I don't give a shit why he did it. He did it and that makes him an asshole, plain and simple."

"Okay, fine," I said. "When we meet next year, we can talk about it and probably something else will happen at Trader Vic's. And I'm sure we'll have some more boring and pretentious presentations."

"Not me. I'm done. This is the last one of these things for me." He picked up the check, walked to the counter, paid the cashier, and left. I never saw him again.

I was going to write him a letter to apologize, but for what? What could I say? All I did at Trader Vic's was tell him not to talk to some stranger who looked like Abbie Hoffman. I was going to tell him about my plan for a long-distance friendship, but the thought made me slightly embarrassed. I was going to call him, but I couldn't imagine why. When the opportunity came for attending the Chicago Conference in 1970, I turned it down. I grew into a competent, responsible, serious English teacher. I had plenty of friends at the school and where I lived. I didn't need one from Mt. Vernon.

I learned about his death in a note from his wife. "Chris," she wrote, "Tim died last week of cancer. He had been retired for a while. He had you on his list of people to contact when he passed away. You two must have met in Chicago years ago. He left teaching in the early '70s and went to work at the hardware store and finally became the manager. I hope you enjoyed teaching. He did mention you from time to time."

I did write her back. I told her I had stayed in teaching at Forest High and finally retired after many, many years, but I am still helping out. I said that I became one of those guys we liked to make fun of—a curriculum director. I didn't add that for a little while I thought we could have been good friends, but it just didn't happen.

The
Caddy

I'm a caddy. I used to work as a runner for guys trading pork bellies and other crap at the Board of Trade, but I hated those people. How can you respect morons in odd-colored jackets squealing and shoving and making silly hand signals? Those guys really thought they were something special. But I knew they weren't. The Exchange was one huge pit full of kids. They were all kids, even the old ones. It makes me want to vomit just to think about them. I could have strangled every one of them.

Now at Pine Acres, where I caddy, you find adults, not guys bent over bathroom sinks cutting lines of coke with their plastic ID cards. You find confident men who move slowly, even when they have somewhere they need to be. And they always smile. They smile at me and the other caddies. They smile at the black guys and the Mexicans who work in the kitchen. They smile at each other. Not big, toothy grins, just simple smiles.

I love everything about the place. That's why I came back. I love standing all alone in the bag room at night. It's dark in there except for a little light reflecting off the metal clubs. It smells of leather and earth. In the whole world, there's nothing like the smell of the bag room at a country club. Once when I was a young caddy, I spent the whole night in the bag room. I waited until my mother was asleep and then I sneaked out of our apartment back to the club and climbed through the window. I curled up next to a huge black leather bag and made a pillow out of some club covers. I still go in there any chance I get. Anyway, I see caddying as real work. And I get to meet the finest people you can find anywhere—people like Mr. Roger Burrows.

There's a picture of Mr. Burrows on the wall of the men's grill. It was taken after a special golfing event. It shows a bunch of men sitting around the pool sipping gin and tonics. Most of them are wearing green pants or yellow pants with light blue blazers. They look tanned and freshly showered. The tables have bowls of chips and smaller containers of dip. A black waiter in a white coat is standing behind. Mr. Burrows is off to the side looking past the men sitting next to him. He's wearing black slacks with a green shirt and a light sport coat.

Mr. Burrows and I knew each other at Forest High School. But after he went to Princeton and I went to work, we didn't see each other. Some time after I had given up the bag the first time, he joined Pine Acres—just like his parents.

"Remember me?" I asked him the first time I caddied for him. We were walking down the fairway of the first hole. I had to hurry to keep up with his long strides.

He slowed down just a bit and turned to look at me. "Arthur? Arthur? My God, of course I do! We played football together in high school." I can still picture myself in that green Pine Acres T-shirt with the big bunker behind me. Mr. Burrows was looking right at me, not at anything else in the whole world.

At thirty-two he was already graying just a bit. But he still looked like the running back I used to block for —broad shoulders, strong jaw, big forearms, deep intense eyes. My mother remembered those eyes. She used to clean his family's house. She said the whole family joked about Roger's eyes. "They're staring all the way from Chicago to Princeton," they'd say.

He asked me if I'd been a caddy for a long time, and I told him how I'd caddied at Pine Acres through high school and that I had come back after my rotten experience at the Exchange. He told me that lots of people our age were caddying. We both shrugged. Then he lowered his voice and kind of smiled and said, "Maybe some day I'll quit the bank and join you."

By now we had reached his drive and I handed him a five iron. We both stopped talking as he lined up the shot. He waggled the club a few times and then started his backswing. He had a nice full swing with a complete follow-through. The ball landed on the green and bounced backward.

For the rest of that round we jabbered on about high school. He said that when we played football, he liked to run to the right because he knew I'd always clear the way for him. He didn't seem surprised that I was still living at home. A few holes later he had me shake hands with the others in the foursome. "If you ever need help, Arthur here is your man," he said. One man in the foursome, a fat bald guy, made a point of not looking at me when he shook my hand.

On the way back to the clubhouse after the 18th hole, I asked if I still could call him Mr. Burrows.

"If that's easier, fine. But I get to call you Arthur."

"That's the way it should be."

On the way to the clubhouse, we talked about his game. If he played in the club championship, he wanted me to carry the bag. He had broken 80 for the first time that summer.

It was that way all summer. If I wasn't out on a loop already, I would caddy for Mr. Burrows. I got to know his game. The four times he shot in the seventies, I was his man. He'd ask for advice, and I'd give it to him. When he was having trouble in the bunkers, I told him to keep his weight forward. On long irons, I had him line up a little bit left and throw his arms out toward the target. I could get him to slow down if he was getting too excited. He would never putt until I had given him my opinion about the green.

What I really liked about Mr. Burrows was that he could see all the way through bullshit. This one time the others in his foursome were talking about alcoholics. I guess someone in the club had just joined a dry-out program or something and had gone off to some place in Minnesota. Then one of the other players came out with the crap you hear all the time about not being able to help someone unless "he wants to be helped." Now if you think about that statement, it's pretty stupid. In the first place, people say it because other people have said it. They haven't really thought up the words themselves. But people still nod and frown like something smart has been said. And it's bullshit. Who says you can't make someone stop drinking? And how can you tell what people *want* to do? Anyway, on this afternoon, this guy frowned, lowered his voice, and announced, "You know, it doesn't do any good to help a drinker unless he wants to be helped." Everyone else—even the other caddies—nodded like pigeons and mumbled. Not Mr. Burrows. He just studied the scorecard and didn't say one word. He might have known my dad was a drinker, who would have been better off if someone had kicked his ass until he stopped.

After caddying, I usually stopped at the Wonder Bar for shots and beer. I didn't have any friends at the club. Most of the caddies were much younger. They wouldn't want to hang out with a thirty-two-year-old. And their parents wouldn't be too hot on the idea either. I'd sit there and drink beer and think about what I had done that day. And I'd always think about Mr. Burrows. Sometimes I'd drive past his house on the way home from the bar so I could imagine his life better. He lived in a big brick place back in the woods. And I knew what his wife and kids looked like because they would hang around the pool. Her name was Henrietta. She was tall and handsome. And I guess very rich. A waitress told me that Mr. Burrows met her at a party on Long Island.

One time I took a short cut from the caddy shack to the parking lot, and on the way I passed the swimming pool. Mr. Burrows and his family were there but sitting off in the corner. She was on a lounge chair reading a big book. Mr. Burrows was sitting on the deck near her. It looked like he was doing a crossword puzzle. The daughters, who were handsome like their mother, were sitting on towels playing cards. No one looked too happy.

In mid-August things slowed down. The weather turned hot and humid. A lot of caddies went back to school. I was often the only guy at the club carrying bags. One afternoon I was watching a ball game in the caddy shack, and Mr. Burrows walked in and came right over to me. "Let's play nine, Arthur," he said. "We'll carry our own bags." I looked at the caddy master, but he just shrugged a "Why not?" and we went off and played. I figured it would be awkward for a few holes, but then it would be fun. I wanted Mr. Burrows to see how far I could drive a golf ball. But he was off somewhere else, and I could barely get him to talk. After seven holes, it started raining, and we left. In the parking lot he apologized for being so gloomy. I said it was gloomy weather. Then we got into our cars and drove away.

In September, Mr. Burrows played a few rounds with a man named Ben Flowers. It seemed strange because Ben was not really Burrows's type—or anyone's, for that matter. In the first place, he had to be at least seventy-five years old. He wore shiny pants. He talked during the game. He had a terrible sense of humor. And he was mean. A few years ago, he got a caddy fired for laughing. My mother never liked working for people like that. She warned me, "Watch out for the mean old men. They'll hurt you." But I bet that prick was a mean young man too. No wonder he never married.

The caddy master told me that Mr. Burrows had worked for Flowers at the First National Bank, and when Flowers retired, he took over most of his accounts. In the winter Flowers lived in some old people's place in Florida; in the summer he stayed in Chicago. This fall he was actually living in an apartment owned by Pine Acres. Even though he and Mr. Burrows belonged to the same club, they looked more like two strangers who happened to be walking alongside each other. They were like people who leave the train together. They have nothing in common except the ride.

The club championship was played the last weekend in September, and Mr. Burrows decided to enter. I thought maybe he had gone East with his family because I hadn't seen his wife and kids at the pool. But it turned out he'd stayed behind, and that's when he started playing golf with Ben Flowers all the time. With almost all of the other caddies gone, I carried their bags every day. They would play at odd times; it seemed like we were the only ones on the course. Once a guy playing alone joined us, but usually it would just be the three of us—Mr. Burrows, Mr. Ben Flowers, and me carrying two bags. Autumn was coming, and the leaves would soon begin to fall, and there's nothing worse than trying to find a golf ball in the leaves.

Things got uncomfortable fast, especially when they started playing for fifty dollars a hole. Sometimes people play for money, but not for that much. But the season was over, so no one would notice anyway. Mr. Burrows was a much better golfer so he had to give Flowers a stroke on practically every hole.

A few days later things took a real ugly turn. As we were walking down the first fairway, Flowers started talking into Mr. Burrow's left ear. He would stop occasionally to spit and then catch up with Mr. Burrows and grab him by the elbow and start jabbering again. I couldn't quite hear what he was saying, but I could hear the old man kind of giggling. Every so often he would poke Mr. Burrows in the ribs and cackle. Once he said something and looked over at me and grinned. I just stared back at the wrinkled little bastard. Mr. Burrows stopped walking and just shook his head. He had a pained look on his face. I really felt sorry for him, but I couldn't do anything. It wasn't like football where I could make the block to spring him loose.

On the back nine that day, Flowers started saying things to me, but he made sure Mr. Burrows heard him. Did I know that Mr. Burrows worked for him when he first came to the bank? Did I know that Mr. Burrows was a real party boy back in the early days? He said "boy" with kind of a smirk. Did I know some of the "special" bars that he used to go to? Had I ever seen any pictures of him dancing? The stuff didn't make any sense to me, but Flowers laughed so hard he was snorting. Mr. Burrows just walked on ahead with his hands stuffed in his pants. I stared at the grass and wished I was somewhere else. At the end of the match Mr. Burrows paid Flowers one hundred dollars and walked off to the parking lot without even saying goodbye to me. That had never happened before.

The nastiness got even worse a few days later. On the first tee Mr. Flowers bumped into me and then stuck his face right into mine. He had yellowish pink skin with dark liver spots. One eye had a lot of mucus in it. And he wore this little gold chain around his chicken neck. He reeked of bourbon and cigarettes. "Arthur, I don't want any more fuckups today. When I'm putting, keep your mouth shut."

I started to say something, but he just laughed and walked away and I stared at the ground. People don't say things like that at our club. And I never talk when people are putting. Mr. Burrows heard it all and tried to make a joke, but he knew how I felt. Flowers must have been drunk, though, because he forgot it right away.

For the rest of the round, he taunted Mr. Burrows. They were playing for even bigger money. Flowers would whisper things during his shots. Once I looked over and they were pointing fingers at each other. I looked back again and Flowers had his arm around Mr. Burrows's shoulder, and Burrows was squirming to get loose. Finally on the 15th hole, Flowers lost his ball in the woods. He claimed he'd found it, but he had obviously dropped another one. I was his caddy, for Christ's sake. I knew he was using a Pinnacle. But he picked up a Titleist that he swore was his. He had a shot to the green and ended up somehow winning the hole. When we were walking to the next green, he was whispering in Mr. Burrows's ear. Then he reached into the pocket of his plaid pants and pulled out a color picture. Mr. Burrows took one look at it and marched off to the clubhouse. Flowers shrugged and said, "I think I'll quit too. Come on, Arthur. Let us follow our man-child back to the bar."

The next day—yesterday—we were on the first tee ready

to play again. Flowers was moving more steadily. They had agreed to play for less money. I had never seen Mr. Burrows play better. After seven holes he was one under par, and I think the pressure was affecting him less than me. I was really excited for him. He was quiet. He made a point of walking down the fairway near me. Flowers was off by himself. One time Flowers cheated, but no one said anything. By the 9th hole, Mr. Burrows had slipped over par, but he was still playing great. At this rate he was going to be in the low seventies.

On hole number 12 he was still just one over par. It was a short hole, just 140 yards. This would be perfect for Mr. Burrows's nine iron. Right before he started to swing, Flowers started talking frantically. "Roger, does Arthur here know that there have been other Arthurs in your life? Have you told him about Terry? Have you told him where you got the money to get darling Terry to vanish?" Flowers had this crazy smirk all over his face. He was leaning on his club in a way that made him look like an old sheepherder. Mr. Burrows stared right at him. His jaw was moving a little. It looked like his eyes were about to explode. He looked down at the ball and then swung wildly. It shot off to the left into the trees, and that was it. He ended up shooting an 84. I felt terrible for him because this was going to be his day.

Afterward, they both went to the bar. I went back to the caddy shack. I was just about to leave when the phone rang.

"Arthur?" It was Mr. Burrows. His voice sounded tight. "I'd like you to do me a favor."

"Of course, sir. Whatever you want."

"Ben and I are going to stay here at the bar for a while. I don't want him driving home. He's already finished off five martinis. I thought it would be better if he left his car here and you walked him home through the woods. He lives in one of those apartments on the other side of the course."

"I know just where it is. A lot of retired members stay over there."

"That's right. Come over to the bar door at ten o'clock. We'll be the only people at the club so it won't look funny for a caddy to be standing there. When we leave, I'll hand you Ben. You can take him by the arm and escort him to the woods. He won't have much to say."

"I'll get him home. No problem."

"One more thing, Arthur." He hesitated for a long time. "I want you to pick up something from my car. It's in the glove compartment. Make sure you do it before you walk him home. Thanks for everything, buddy. You're the best person I know."

I knew where Mr. Burrows parked his Lexus. I looked to make sure no one thought I was breaking in. Then I opened the passenger door and sat down. The car had a warm, leathery feeling to it. It reminded me of the bag room. It was empty except for some books in the backseat. I guess Mr. Burrows liked to read. I pushed the button of the glove compartment. The little door came down slowly the way they do on good cars. On my cars they always flopped down like they have been dropped from the sky. Inside I could see the title to the Lexus, the insurance forms, and some maps. Below the maps something glistened. It was a hunting knife, and even before I touched it, I knew it would be razor-sharp.

London
101

As young teachers with no children and later as not-so-young teachers with no children, my wife and I spent our summer vacations happily traveling. For the most part we avoided group tours not because we felt superior, but because we could do quite well on our own, thank you. After all, we were dependable social studies teachers from Forest

High School. We could take care of ourselves. In fact my nickname at Forest High—well-earned—was "Dependable Ben." Or just plain "Debendable."

But then I retired and, just like that, decided a group trip with a bunch of strangers might not be such a bad idea. Instead of staying home alone while my wife visited her sister in Portland, I would take a two-week "Discovery" tour to London. This would be my first act as a retired person. Now other people could take over part of my life. At least that's what I told my wife, who asked me why I was visiting a place I had been to five times with a bunch of sixty-five-year-old insurance salesmen. "That's what I want," I responded confidently. But as the day for leaving drew closer, I did begin to wonder why I was really taking this trip. I had to admit to myself that I didn't really know, but that was the fun of it—I guess.

All of us on the tour gathered together at O'Hare Airport, United Gate C9, and waited for Flight 431 to London Heathrow. Lots of handshakes and introductions. Bankers, insurance salesmen and adjusters, a lawyer, a barber, a limo driver. I was the only teacher and the only one who had already been to London. (I didn't let on that I had been there five times.) So, right away the group let me have it. "Why are you going back?" ("It's been a while. It's like visiting an old friend.") "What about the subway?" ("Call it the tube.") "Crime?" ("I've never had a problem, but be careful.") "Food?" ("It's getting better.") "Weather?" ("Get an umbrella.") "Favorite places?" ("The National Portrait Gallery and the War Museum.") Good, solid, dependable answers.

Later, on the plane, I sat next to a guy from our group. He was a slightly overweight, retired sales rep for a dental supply company. He showed me a list of Jeopardy-style trivia questions. He read the answers and I came up with the questions.

Answer: Guy Fawkes. Question: Who tried to blow up the Parliament?

Answer: Camilla. Question: What's the first name of Prince Charles's second wife?

Answer: Gaol. Question: How do the British spell "jail"?

Easy stuff, but this fellow—whose name was Rex—decided I was a real scholar.

Then it was reading, snoozing, and eating bad plane food. With a few minutes left in the flight, I shared something I knew he'd like. "Rex," I said, "the English some-times say, 'Keep your pecker up.'"

"They do? Why?" He leaned toward me, stretching his seatbelt.

"It doesn't mean what you think it does. It actually means 'be brave' or 'be strong' or 'don't give up.'"

"Thanks, Ben," he said, "I'll remember that."

"You might need to," I said, and we shared a good laugh.

After passing through customs and picking up our bags, we moved as a group out into a large area and right away spotted a short, stocky, middle-aged man with a red face and a sign: "London Adventures, Limited." He was our guy. "Hello, Yanks," he called out with a huge smile and a London accent. "My name is Graham. I'll be your man for the next two weeks." Even though it was summer, he was wearing a suit and vest. He read our names from a list on a clipboard he was carrying. "All present and accounted for," he said. "Let's get on the bus, and make sure to say hi to Nigel."

Nigel, it turned out, was the bus driver. He smiled as we passed. A few people even shook his hand. Whoever heard of shaking the bus driver's hand? But it seemed right. Just like the group seemed right. I sat down next to Herb, a retired CPA from Toledo, and prepared to look out the window. I couldn't help thinking this was really okay. Tours make it easy. Maybe that's the point. When you're retired, easy is what matters most.

But instead of looking out the window, I found myself staring at a sheet of paper that Graham passed out to each of us: "The Graham Plan." It featured a hand-drawn map of London with numbers. The numbers referred to places we would visit—the usual places: Buckingham Palace, Westminster Abbey, Speakers' Corner, the National Gallery, Parliament, the Tower of London, St. Paul's. While we read, he chattered on about what was in store for us. "Maybe you can get one of the guards at Buckingham to smile." "Don't end up in the Tower prison."

Obviously, Graham wanted to get off to a good start, and why not? He wanted to earn his money. He wanted us to pass on the good word that this little company, London Adventures, had a capable person running the show.

Then he told us what we already knew from the brochure we had received in the mail: each day would be devoted to an "exploration" of a few specific places; we'd have time on our own in the afternoon. We were staying in a hotel on

Russell Square and the British Museum was nearby. "You could spend the rest of your life there."

Finally he announced, "I'll shut up now. You can look out the window at London on one of our rare sunny days. You can actually see shadows!"

We all nodded and mumbled approvingly. I even considered a quick nap before getting to the hotel. The traffic was awful. But then Dottie, an older lady sitting across the aisle from me who was traveling by herself, shouted out, "Graham, you're the best. I can tell already you're a wonderful teacher. Too bad our schools don't have more people like you." Others chimed in. There was even some applause. The others looked back at me, the real teacher, and I gave them the thumbs up.

I applauded too, but I have to admit that I was a tiny bit annoyed. Was Dottie serious? Are characters like Graham really the solution to our schools' problems? I felt myself getting pissed at myself for being so petty. Who gives a shit what this lady says? I've been petty many times. We all have. But I couldn't recall being so conscious of my own pettiness and my inability to make it go away.

But I tried.

But the next day, I got angry again for a little while. It started when several people started calling Graham "Professor" and then they'd look at me for approval. He looked embarrassed at first, but I could tell he kind of liked it. That's what really got to me, but I just smiled and did the same thing. I called him "Professor," even though he reminded me more of a music hall entertainer.

That day Nigel drove us past the "Biggies," as Graham called them, and after a while I was relaxed and enjoying the sights from my comfortable seat on the bus. At Buckingham Palace, Graham pointed out where the person had scaled the wall and climbed into the Queen's bedroom. When we passed Whitehall, he pointed to a building and told us that below there, in a secured spot, Prime Minister Winston Churchill and his aides had planned strategy for the war. "Imagine how tense that must have been," he said. "No wonder Winston needed booze to relax. Lots of booze, from what I've heard." We all smiled, but Brian Gibbs, a lawyer in our group from Iowa, laughed louder and longer than anyone else. Obviously, he wanted us to know how funny he thought that was. "Not my type," I muttered to myself. "Not my type."

By the third day, I was getting used to the "Professor" nonsense, but Lawyer Gibbs was still getting on my nerves. He reminded me of all those loud, rude, shallow students who sat in the back row and scowled.

At lunch the third day, Gibbs threw down several pints of Guinness and then began to sound off about schools. Not a particular school, but "schools," as if anyone could talk about them in such a general way. He's a lawyer. He should know better. But that didn't stop him, and he directed his rant right at me. "Dottie was right," he blathered, "schools could use more people like Graham. American schools are just plain awful," he said. "The only solution is more charter schools. We have to offer merit pay. We have to get rid of the tenure system. Common Core is where it's at."

Now, of course, he was drunk, but still, how stupid can you get? And why make an outburst on a trip like this? But he finished and glowered at me, and the rest of the group looked over to see what I was going to do. The trouble was, I am not that quick on my feet. I'm not a debater. Instead of a clever comeback, I stammered and then muttered something about schools being more "complicated" than people realize.

"Don't I know it," Gibbs half-shouted. "My aunt has been a teacher in the public schools her whole adult life. She agrees with everything I say." With that, he nodded and turned back to his Guinness and I hurried over to the gents' room and then headed for the bus.

The next morning at breakfast, Gibbs came over to where I was sitting and apologized for his drunken tirade. I accepted his apology and told him, in a loud voice that I hoped others could hear, that later on maybe we could talk a bit. I'd be glad to tell him what I learned about teaching from my years at Forest. He nodded and agreed that would be a good idea, and that was it.

We left the hotel and climbed on the bus and headed for Westminster Abbey. This proved to be Graham at his most flamboyant. We hurried past the gravestones of Jane Austen, the Brontës, and other famous people, and stood in the front looking back. "Imagine two thousand people. That's how many were here for Princess Di's funeral. Steven Spielberg sat there. Tom Cruise was over there near Nelson Mandela. Tony Blair read from Corinthians. Elton John played." (Graham actually sang at this point.) "I watched it at home with my family. Billions of people watched. It was one of the most watched events in history. And you should see the movie *The Queen*."

On the way out, we walked past more famous graves. "Ben," he asked, "anything to add?"

I just nodded and gave him the thumbs up. "You're doing fine, Professor." In fact, I could have added some details, but why bother?

In the afternoon, I visited the National Portrait Gallery on my own. This is my favorite London place of all. I spent a lot time in front of the portraits of Benjamin Disraeli and Mick Jagger, listening on my headset to wonderfully insightful talk about the people themselves and the artists who painted them.

That night at dinner I shared this Portrait Gallery experience with the people at my table. They nodded politely and asked a few questions. But not much interest. The man from Toledo actually got up and left as I was describing the portrait of Princess Diana. I was annoyed. Who wouldn't have been? But I stayed calm and that was it.

But I guess I must have been angrier than I thought, considering what I did the next day. It happened in Islington, a neighborhood twenty minutes from central London. It was once a rural suburb. Artists and writers have lived there. I had taken a walking tour a few years ago and remembered quite a bit.

Graham spent the little time we had talking about the buildings. He showed us where Orwell lived when he wrote *1984*. We went to a house that looked out on grazing land. He explained that the people did not want to look at fences, so they dug a long ditch and put the fence down there, out of sight. He asked if we knew the name of that ditch. I did and I shouted louder than necessary, "It's called a ha-ha." They all turned and looked at me. Graham laughed and applauded and said, "Good job, Ben. You've done your homework." I was embarrassed that I had been so exuberant. I was angry because Graham had talked down to me. I was aware that Gibbs was grinning in that asshole way of his. I could see the group turning back to Graham for more knowledge. They were not the least bit impressed that I knew that a trench with a fence at the bottom is called a ha-ha. I'm sure they were all thinking, "What kind of a loser knows what a ha-ha is?"

Two things happened. One, I started feeling incredibly separate from the group to the point that I thought of walking off and grabbing the tube back to Russell Square and packing my suitcase and taking a taxi to Heathrow and flying back to Chicago. The second thing was that I noticed we were on Noel Road, and I suddenly remembered what had happened on Noel Road in 1967. I had been here before. I'm a history teacher. I remember things.

As the group started moving away with Graham in the lead, I shouted and they looked back at me. "Graham," I yelled, "you forgot something. You forgot what happened in this house in 1967."

Graham looked at me. "I guess I forgot. But why don't you tell us, Ben?" Once again, he was using that patronizing voice.

And I did. I told them that Joe Orton, the playwright, had lived in a house on Noel Road in the '60s. His career was just taking off. He was about to break up with his boyfriend, a man named Kenneth Halliwell. Then one night in August of 1967, something awful took place.

They were all silent, wondering what I was going to say. "Kenneth was furious. He didn't want his lover to leave. He brought a hammer with him and bludgeoned Joe Orton to death. He hit him nine times! Nine times on the head." I acted out a man hitting his lover on the head with a hammer. "Then Kenneth took a bottle full of pills and died right next to Orton."

Graham looked stricken. He turned and hustled away and the group followed. All but Gibbs. He hurried up to me and put a hand on my shoulder. "Hey, Ben, let's go back to the hotel. I was going to leave early anyway."

I glared and shrugged and followed him to the station. The group had turned to watch me, but no one said a thing.

That night I stayed up in my room. I didn't want to go to dinner. I was still angry, but also embarrassed. How could I not be embarrassed? No one did things like that. I never in my life had done anything like that. For the rest of their lives, these ordinary people would remember when this bland ex-schoolteacher had told them about the bloody death of Joe Orton.

Graham came up to my room later on. He sat down on my bed, and we talked. I apologized over and over. I told him I hadn't slept. I was tired. I missed my wife. I was still angry with Gibbs, but I was really sorry.

"I bet you were one of those quiet teachers that kids respected. You got papers done on time. You were fair but not flashy."

"Something like that."

"This would have been a good chance to show your stuff. No wonder I pissed you off."

"That's not what happened."

"Not to worry," he said, "you're part of the family. That's how I always think of my tour groups. I've done this for twenty years. Now, come on down for coffee and dessert. If you don't, the group will think something's really wrong. Plus, we have to talk about the trip tomorrow. Nigel's driving us to Hampton Court."

"Will we have time to walk through the the maze?" I was relieved to switch the conversation from me.

"Of course."

In the dining room, people were finishing their desserts. Several looked up and smiled. Rex stood up and walked toward me. "Hey, Ben, you forget to keep your pecker up."

Coach

I could never make up my mind if Mr. Miles Manning looked old or young. Up close you could see the wrinkles and spots on his hands and face. And loose skin hung from his neck. And he had dark marks under his eyes. But from across the field he looked like a young guy with red hair. And he acted young, too, because he was really kind of simple. He was probably the simplest adult I had ever met. Not stupid—just simple. Whatever happened, he'd just smile and shrug.

People at Forest High called him "Coach" even though he had coached only one year as assistant for the sophomore football team, and that was ten years ago. My brother was on that team and said Manning didn't know the difference between a field goal and a fair catch. Most of the time he'd walk around with that dopey smile on his face saying things like, "Go get 'em, guys. Go get 'em." In one game he actually cheered when the other team scored a touchdown. When that happened, even the cheerleaders froze. Instead of apologizing or making up an excuse, he just shrugged. My brother said it was like it didn't matter to him, or if it did, he couldn't do anything. I heard that was the last day he ever coached at Forest High.

But everyone still called him "Coach," even though he was nothing more than a PE flunky. His job title was some kind of assistant. Before class, he took roll. When we had swimming, he passed out towels. When we played touch football, he moved the yard-line markers. If the teacher in charge forgot something, Coach would hustle back to get it. "Manning, I forgot the bases. Run and get them, okay?"

"Go, Coach," we'd all shout and off he'd sprint. He loved to run. Most of the time he would take the long way around. A few minutes later, we'd see him tearing toward us with his arms full of bases, and we'd give another big cheer.

But even though he seemed really stupid when he sprinted across the field, he looked happy and relaxed. I'd call it *easy*—everything about Coach was easy. He was supposed to be a smart guy. He came to Forest as a history teacher. My brother said he knew a lot about Lincoln and the people you study in American history. One time he brought in a World War II hand grenade. Another time he brought in a letter written by Teddy Roosevelt. He also wrote articles for some teacher magazine. But he couldn't make the kids shut up. I guess they didn't want to fire him, so they reassigned him to the PE department. Right after they took away his job, my brother saw him alone in his old classroom. The lights were out, and he had all of his teaching stuff on his desk, and he was staring out the window.

But he was an odd dude. Last year he caught up with me as we were walking back to the locker room across the football field.

"Archie, I've got to ask you something," he said. He had noticed I was wearing a shirt with a picture of the blues singer Koko Taylor. That really excited him. He told me that two summers ago he had dropped off his wife with her family in Indiana and driven all by himself through the Mississippi Delta where a lot of those old blues singers had lived. He knew what to look for because he had read a book about the old singers. He even played blues music in the car. He asked me if I loved the blues as much as he did. I said I didn't know anything about music and that the shirt belonged to my brother. Coach frowned, but then he gave me a big nod and a smile, and I smiled back. From that time on, he made a point of calling me "Koko."

When you got to be an upperclassman at Forest, you got to make fun of Coach. You couldn't do it as a freshman, but by the time you were a junior, it was cool. People copied the way he stood with his hands on his hips and rolled his head, looking up at the sky where there was nothing to see. They spoke in his high, scratchy voice. They threw a ball the way he did—just like a girl. Rick Babson was the best impersonator by far. Rick was this big, blond kid on his way to Yale, and even though he didn't look like Coach, he could still do a perfect imitation. He'd drop his shoulders and walk with his feet out. He would gesture in a big, silly kind of way. We'd crack up every time.

Coach must have known what was going on. Some guys would actually speak in his voice when he was nearby. And during games, people would break off into Manning runs. Even the coaches. Sometimes, when it got really bad, he would make his stupid smile even bigger and go off to fiddle with a base or check the pressure of the soccer balls, just to look busy. Mostly he acted like he got it, that everyone was laughing *with* him and not *at* him.

I could copy him, too, but I wasn't very good at making fun of people. And, to tell you the truth, it was hard to make fun of him because I knew he liked me. This was obvious ever since he told me about the blues. He didn't say much, but I would catch him looking at me. Once in a touch football game, he listened in on the other team's huddle and then nodded at the guy who was going to catch the pass. When I made the interception on the next play, Coach clapped and everyone hooted. It gave me a really creepy feeling inside. Another time he stopped me in the hall to tell me that when he retired in two years, his wife said he could study music in the city.

"I think he's queer for you, Archie," Weldon shouted one day driving home. He had to shout because the muffler of his van was shot. "He's always looking at you. You'd better be careful in the shower." We were driving near the projects. Weldon went this way when he wanted to buy weed. He didn't tell me that's why he stopped at the old apartment building and went inside, but I knew.

I wasn't considered a real pot smoker, so supposedly I didn't know how things worked. If someone brought out a joint at a party, I might take a hit, but that was it. I wasn't into the whole business of buying and selling. And it wasn't that big a deal, anyway. We were just kids getting ready to go off to college and having fun our senior year.

Actually, I wasn't going off to college because I would be staying home to run the family restaurant, Dominick's. My dad dropped dead when I was a freshman, and I was the one to keep the place going because my brother and his family lived in California. We all thought it would be great if I worked during the day and went to community college at night. That was fine with me. I wouldn't have been going to a good college anyway.

I was a good fit for the restaurant. My hair was starting to recede a little bit, and I had started to call adults by their first names. Rudy the barber had even asked me to join a bowling league.

One time Coach and his wife came into the restaurant.

I looked up from my *Sports Illustrated* and saw Mrs. Manning heading for a table in the back with Coach following along. It was the kind of place where people just walked in and sat down at one of the tables or at the counter. The table where they sat had no window, but there was a large poster of the Italian Alps. Coach read the menu, and she sat there with her head slightly bowed. She was small like Coach, but she looked firm. Whenever I saw her around town, she was always wearing plain colors and had her hair pulled back like a pioneer woman. My mom said that Mrs. Manning worked in a hospital in the city and that she had grown up in a religious community in Indiana.

Coach had a cheeseburger, and Mrs. Manning ordered a garden salad. During the meal he took out a map and leaned it against the napkin holder so that they both could see it. After they finished eating, they were standing by the counter. She had just paid the bill, and he had been standing off to the side looking at a picture of the restaurant that had been taken twenty years ago. "Frieda," he suddenly spoke up, "this young man is Archie Ori. He's a senior at the high school."

Mrs. Manning stopped fussing with her change purse and looked right at me. "Hello, Archie." She spoke clearly.

"And whom are you named after?" She tipped her head and stared into my face. From that angle, I could see that she wasn't wearing earrings.

It was an odd question, but I tried to answer it. "My grandfather was named Archibald, so I guess that's why. He came here from Italy."

"And whom was he named after? Archie is an unusual name for Italians." For a second I thought she was going to take notes. When I told her I didn't know, she frowned. Then she smiled and reached over the counter to shake my hand. "Nice to meet you, Archie Ori. Whoever you are. Come on, Miles. We have to do more weeding before it gets dark." Out the door she marched with Coach hustling to keep up. But he did look back at me with one of his simple smiles. And naturally he shrugged.

They lived in a small house about two blocks away. It backed up on a huge field where people grew vegetables. Mrs. Manning could walk everywhere from there. And she would catch the train to the hospital. As I watched them leave, I wondered if she had any idea how often the kids made fun of her husband.

The Hartmut Incident happened in the spring, a few weeks before graduation. We had this exchange student from Dusseldorf named Hartmut Wuhlrob, and he was a complete dork. In fact, we made fun of him as much as we made fun of Coach, and I would join in, too. He would say things like "waycation," when he meant "vacation," and he wore his pants too high. And he could never quite figure out what we were talking about.

But he did figure out that we liked to make fun of Coach. One day we were lying down between halves of a soccer game when all of a sudden, this goofy German leaped up and crouched over us and started chattering in what he must have thought was a Manning voice. And he did all of this right in front of Coach. And when Coach tried to get away, Hartmut actually chased him and kept on jabbering. It was sickening.

Well, Babson went nuts. That wasn't the way we did things. He walked up to Hartmut and shoved him down right beside a soccer goal. "If you do that any more, you fucking Kraut, I'll punch your pig eyes into your skull." Hartmut lay on the ground stammering in German. We were in a semicircle, hoping that they would fight. And off to the side with his mouth opening and closing stood Coach. For just a second I thought he was going to say something, but instead he stared at his hands and kept moving his lips.

Then he turned and tore across the fields right through the middle of a freshman soccer game, into the parking lot and headed toward his house. Some students standing next to a car and smoking leaped out of the way when they saw him coming. They said his face was wild, not like it usually was at all.

Coach didn't come to school those last two weeks before everything closed down for the summer. I didn't see him in the hall. Someone said he had called in sick. Someone else said they heard shouting from his house.

We had a small party in the restaurant the day after graduation. My mom let the kids drink if they promised to walk home. She also stayed in the front of the restaurant so she didn't have to catch anyone smoking pot in the back alley. We did adult things like shaking hands and hugging. My friends wished me good luck with my job and community college. I'm sure they didn't believe me when I said I was glad that I was staying home. Toward the end of the evening Babson staggered in with an older girl. He had lipstick on his face. The girl's blouse was buttoned wrong. He was loaded but still sharp enough to do one of his best Coach impersonations. Then someone suggested we call Coach, but I vetoed that idea. Someone else said they had seen him in town and that he looked like an old man. "He didn't even have that dumb smile. He just walked right by me like a zombie." And he was always alone—in the summer his wife visited her family in Indiana.

When he did come into the restaurant that summer, he barely said hello. Strangers must have thought he was some kind of street person because his shirt wasn't tucked in and he needed a shave. He'd shuffle in and head for a table in the back. He'd have a book, but instead of reading it, he would just stare at the tabletop. Once I walked over to his table and tried to start a conversation about black singers, but he just nodded. "When does Mrs. Manning get back from Indiana?" I asked before I walked back to my place behind the counter.

"It's hard to say." He didn't look up. "Her sisters need her down there to help with the farm." He wasn't going to say anything more. Man, he looked sad. I thought that she had to be pretty mean to leave him like this.

I played catcher on a softball team that summer. In the second game I hit a home run. When I crossed home plate, I saw Coach in the crowd, but he wasn't cheering. I also signed up for my community college courses. At the time I thought for a second about asking Coach for advice in picking out classes. But then I could see how lame that would look.

I also spent more time with my mom. Now that I was an adult, it was okay to do things like that. We would sit in the living room of our apartment with the TV on. She always sat in the same chair where she could see the picture of my brother with the other members of the National Honor Society. There was also a picture of my father accepting the Class B golf championship trophy at the local course. Like lots of golfers, he was a short and stocky guy. When that picture was taken, he hadn't told any of us that he had a bad heart. Maybe he didn't know. Mom still wore her wedding ring, but she had to get it fixed to fit her skinny fingers because she had lost a lot of weight since he died. All she really wanted to talk about was the restaurant. Should we hire a new cook? What about expanding? Would it be a good idea for me to take some restaurant management courses in college? These were probably the same things she said to my dad when he was alive. I didn't ask what she thought about all those times she was alone.

Toward the end of July, I saw Coach gardening. He was on his knees weeding in this place he had cleared out. It looked like he planned to plant something. He and Mrs.

Manning were supposed to have a spectacular garden, but it looked a little sickly to me, especially with that big bare spot.

"How are you doing, Coach?" I called out and walked over to him. He stood up and shook my hand.

"Nice to see you, Archie." He actually smiled a little. "How's business at your restaurant?" He was wearing a baggy blue jogging suit that was big enough for Babson.

"Business is great. We had to hire a new dishwasher. Next year the Rotary Club will start meeting at our place." I was really glad to see him.

"That's got to make you and your mom happy." He started to smile a little bit more.

"You know it does. I've also started doing some of the cooking." I felt like talking, and he seemed kind of interested, so I told him that my brother was coming to town in a month.

"I knew him. Isn't his name Dominick, just like your Dad? He's the one who gave you the Koko Taylor shirt." This was the first time I had seen that stupid grin for quite a while. And it made me feel good. I had forgotten what it was like to be around Coach. "When he was on the sophomore football team, I was one of the assistants. You must have heard that I cheered for the other team one time." He looked off in the distance toward the school. From where we were standing you could see the smokestack and part of the field. I could even see the place by the soccer goal where Babson had threatened to punch out Hartmut's eyes.

"When he gets to town, I'll let you know. I know he'd like to see you. When you come to the restaurant, we can all talk." I felt myself slipping into an adult voice. This was the kind of thing adults did—making plans to get together.

But he wasn't really listening anymore. He had gone back to his knees and was pulling out weeds. "Maybe so, Archie." His voice was faint and hard to understand. "Maybe so. But I might be gone. I have two more weeks to decide if I'm coming back."

"Coach, you can't retire!"

"I can still take early retirement. It might be time for me to do some more traveling." He had found a way to turn his back on me. He had stopped pulling at the ground. I didn't really want to see the expression on his face.

"I have lots of work here," he said. And then, just before I started walking back to town, he looked right at me and said, "Archie, you're a lucky man." I stood there and then walked off.

My brother came and went. We drove to a Cubs game in the city. I bicycled with his kids over to the high school so they could see where their father had been an athlete and an honor student. My brother's wife helped in the kitchen. She even prepared one of the specials: "Anne's Mighty Meatloaf." On their last day, she took my mother to the mall and bought her three new outfits. Up until this trip, I had called her "my brother's wife." Now I called her my "sister-in-law." And then they flew back to San Diego. I hadn't even mentioned Coach.

Then late that August I stopped by Coach's house. He didn't answer after I rang the doorbell, but I could hear him shuffling inside, so I didn't go anywhere. Finally he opened the door about a foot and peered out. He blinked. His skin was white, and his eyes were pink. He looked really old. He was wearing the same jogging suit that he wore gardening, but it looked even bigger. His hair hadn't been cut. I could see some gray in the corners. It had never occurred to me that maybe he dyed it red.

"Archie? What are you doing here?"

"Can I come in?" I had never been inside his house. We all imagined it to be plain and clean, just like his wife. It wouldn't have trophies or family pictures. Before today, I hadn't wanted to see it because it might show me what a depressing guy Coach really was.

"Not today, Archie." His voice was flat and dry. "The house is a mess. I'm packing up." I got this feeling if I tried to barge in, he would block the way.

"It's time to go then?" My voice sounded low and far away.

"Oh, yes. It's time to go." He opened the door a little wider, but not much. "I told the principal I wanted early retirement. Schools love that, you know. Now they can hire some new teacher for much less money. I didn't do anything, anyway." His feet were fidgeting. He smelled different, odd. Like an old man, I guess. I had never seen such an unhappy looking human being.

"That day Babson got so mad at the German, that did it, didn't it? That was the day you decided not to come back?"

"That was a bad day. The worst. But I've had some bad days. You have no idea." I could still picture him with that stunned expression looking at Babson and the German.

"How does Mrs. Manning feel about you retiring? Did you get in touch with her in Indiana?"

"She's not coming back, Archie. I sent her away." He cleared his throat and leaned against the door.

"Will you see her again?" Any kids pedaling by on their bikes or people walking with their dogs would have no idea what was happening on the front porch of this little man's house.

"I'll stop and see her in Indiana. She'll show me the church where she works. Then I'll drive south and look for a job." He stood up straighter. He wanted me to leave.

My hands were tingling. Sweat was starting to sneak down my arm. Finally I shook his hand and put my arm around him. Man, did he have bony shoulders.

Brothers

Monty deeply enjoyed the notion that *he* had become the businessman and that Joe—big, burly brother Joe—was the English teacher. After all, Monty had been an English major at Dartmouth and still looked and acted like a teacher—fragile and bookish and a bit of a nitpicker and certainly capable of handling Faulkner without SparkNotes.

But along the way, Monty became a numbers freak at Dartmouth, and that led to an MBA, and that led to a solid career as a banker. Attractive wife, engaged kids, who flew through Forest High with high grades and worthwhile activities.

Monty owned a comfortable house with a sensible swimming pool. He was active at Forest High, where he had served on the school board and several advisory committees, including the BOSS Club (Boys Organization for School Spirit). He thoroughly liked keeping up with life at Forest High, and that included stopping by the English department to see how things were going with Joe and Joe's colleagues.

But at work, when it was time to daydream, Monty would savor even more thoroughly the irony of his big little brother—the one-time state wrestling champion—not only teaching English at the high school, but also doing a pretty darn good job of it.

In college Joe earned a degree in Physical Education. When it was time to look for a job, Monty told him about an opening at his old high school. He got the job, did well, and, to the surprise of his family, on his own at night completed enough graduate teaching courses to earn a teaching certificate in English.

Before Joe knew it, he was teaching basic English classes to noncollege-bound Forest High students. Monty boasted that English departments—hell, all organizations—needed men like his brother. He was just as valuable as the big shots who taught the AP kids and delivered speeches at the National Council of Teachers of English conventions.

Joe lived by himself in a little place near the school. Along with books and teacher stuff, he had some weightlifting trophies and posters of his favorite athletes, especially those from the Green Bay Packers. Joe loved the Packers.

He had a set of keys to the school building, and he knew how the school furnace worked and sometimes was called in to fix it. He watched Monty's house when Monty and his family took trips. He used to help Monty's kids with their homework. He came over for holidays. But he had his own friends in the city.

Still, whenever people asked, "How did that big galoot end up grading themes and leading field trips, and how did you end up worrying about people's money?" Monty would just grin and say, "That's just how things happen, and isn't it great that they do." If they asked if he had helped

Joe get the job, he would say no, Joe got it on his own. But not everyone believed this.

One day at the bank, Monty got a call from the school that he could not believe: Joe had up and quit. He was no longer a teacher at Forest High. Evidently he had stormed out of a department meeting, slamming the door behind him. He had charged down the hall and into the English department. He went right to his desk and collected some things. He scribbled a note to a couple of friends and ran to the parking lot. When he got to his truck, he stopped and waited for the people who were watching this to come within earshot. "Folks, I'm done with this place. I quit. I will not be back. You'd better find someone to replace me." And then he left.

His neighbors reported that he came home and packed his car with boxes and suitcases and drove off. He had not come back.

Two days later, Joe e-mailed Monty to say he was all right. Not to worry. It was something he had to do. Maybe someday he would reconnect, or maybe not. But for now he was gone, gone, gone.

At first, Monty was stunned. Absolutely stunned. This

was something he never expected. Joe, if nothing else, was predictable. Monty was even more stunned when he heard what had happened the afternoon Joe drove off. Right after the meeting had started, Joe stood up and confronted the new department chair, Lucy Barnes. Was it true she was going to change the curriculum to make it more gender and racially aware? Was it true that she was going to have workshops that dealt with "White Privilege"? Was it true that she was going to hire new teachers who were more aware of issues pertaining to social justice? She said it was all true and why didn't he sit down and listen, but instead he headed for the door.

Joe could not imagine his brother worrying about such matters. And for him to stand up as he did was astonishing. He might have joined forces with others, but to leap to his feet and scream and then to leave and never come back? That was not Joe.

But before long, Monty's amazement miraculously melted into admiration. Maybe that *was* Joe. How great to have a brother who would do something like that! How great. Even though, in truth, Monty thought Lucy's ideas made sense and were a long time in coming and could be modified, he was also proud that Joe would do this. People would never forget this. It would mark the calendar—before Joe's outburst and after. People would all claim to have been there. People would say they could see it coming.

But then Monty got a call from Wally French, a local guy who had also served on the school board and who knew someone who knew someone who had heard that Joe and Lucy, apparently married to someone in the city, had been sleeping together. Apparently she had broken things off with Joe when she was promoted to department chair. Joe, the simple man of principles, had turned into the jilted lover.

Time for Monty to be surprised once again. How could his own brother do this without him knowing? What was this about a husband in the city? He had always figured that Lucy was a lesbian. But, in time, as the story spread, Monty was oddly pleased to have a brother who could do that sort of thing. He didn't condone it, but privately he was glad his brother could act on his feelings. Joe could make love and he could get angry. What's wrong with that?

Then a week later when Monty was mowing the lawn, a small gray car pulled into his driveway. He turned off the mower and walked over as Lucy Barnes, a compact forty-year-old, jumped out of the car. She shook his hand. "We need to talk. Should we stay here or go to Starbucks?"

Monty thought Starbucks would be better, and they climbed into her car. His hands were shaking just a little. No small talk on the way over, and this was just as well because he wasn't sure he could keep his voice from trembling.

Monty ordered coffees at the counter and brought them back to where they were sitting. Lucy began in earnest. She knew all about Monty's longtime association with the school—the board, the Booster Club, his kids, friends, and relatives. She knew, of course, that he and Joe were brothers. She knew he would be concerned and no doubt upset by all that had happened.

He agreed. It was true, he was still getting used to his brother being gone. He was glad that they had found a competent replacement for him at Forest High. He hoped one day his brother would come back. In the meantime, Joe was working as a sub in Seattle. The teacher/coach combination made him an attractive candidate. Joe appreciated that Lucy had given him a good recommendation, in spite of what had happened. But yeah, Monty was still concerned by how things had turned out. Maybe she could fill him in.

She sipped her coffee. "The year's about to end, and I

thought we should talk. Things need to be said."

"You are coming back, right?" Monty suddenly imagined that she might be leaving. This had been too much for her. She might be chasing after Joe.

"Oh, I'm coming back, all right. I'm coming back."

"Summer must be a good time to think things over."

"It is, but I'm all set for next year. I have the new classes. We'll have a couple of workshops to facilitate the changes I want. A few teachers are taking early retirement."

Not surprising, Monty thought. The new sheriff was getting her own people.

"I knew your brother would not agree with my changes. We were lovers you know," she announced matter-of-factly. "We talked about those things a lot. Your brother used to tease me about being so politically correct. I teased him about being shallow and thick and juvenile. He liked adventure stories, and I liked stories that got people thinking. I believe deeply that English classes should advance ideas."

"You and my brother actually talked about that?"

"We did—especially after we'd made love. Picture your down-to-earth, uncomplicated jock brother and me, the determined liberal, lying naked on his bed under the picture of Aaron Rodgers and good-naturedly taunting each other. And then we'd make love again. It was great. But then we ended it. It wasn't going to help our careers. Plus, I had second thoughts about dumping my husband."

"And then you got promoted."

"And then I got promoted and then we had that meeting and then your brother went nuts."

"Why then? Couldn't he have waited?"

"We had stopped seeing each other, and he was a little hurt. He certainly would not like taking orders from his ex-girlfriend, especially with ideas he couldn't tolerate. He was angrier than I thought. Maybe he wanted to hurt me. Who knows?"

"Why are you telling me this?"

"As I said, I wanted you to know what was really going on and also to tell you that your brother loved you very much. He was proud of your success. He was proud that you were proud of him. But he wanted out. It turns out I gave him a chance."

Then she stood up. She didn't say good-bye. She didn't ask Monty if he wanted a ride home. She must have known he'd want to walk.

The
Replacement

Mickey was puzzled. Why would a golf coach—of all people—smoke a pipe? But that's exactly what the Ridgefield coach was doing. There he was, in his blue school jacket with a red buffalo emblazoned on the front, puffing away. You'd think this guy—whose name was something like Spalding—was lounging in a pub in Oxford, England, not in the coffee shop at the Peabody Public Links.

He puffed and frowned and then he leaned forward, almost knocking over his Styrofoam cup as he fiddled with the packets of ketchup. "Mickey," he said looking straight ahead, "all of us coaches were surprised to see they named you head golf coach at Forest. You've got quite an act to follow, my boy. Coach Gus set the bar awfully high. What about Simmons? Wasn't he next in line?"

Coach Gus was Gus Walters. Three weeks ago, he was driving a golf cart out to the 8th hole to check up on one of his freshman hotshots. On the way there, he had a massive heart attack and toppled out of the cart onto the grass. He died next to a fairway bunker. Two days later, twenty-eight-year-old Mickey Moran was named to replace him.

Mickey looked back at Coach Spalding, whose team almost always lost out to Forest. "Charlie Simmons left teaching to sell insurance in Santa Fe. I was named Gus's assistant coach, and now I'm the head coach. What can I say?"

"Ever coach golf before? You're a young guy. I hear you teach math to fuckups." Now Spalding was scooping his pipe into an oversized baggy filled with tobacco.

"I coached at a Catholic school in Rochester, and I've played golf all my life. I think I can do it." Last month, he had told the same lies to the athletic director who had interviewed him for the assistant's job. The AD was seriously skeptical, but what was he going to do? He needed someone to collect the scorecards and ride the bus with the younger golfers. Assistant golf coach was basically a flunky's job.

And that had been perfect for Mickey. Forest High required teachers to participate in one activity. Now he could quit as assistant drama director, which had called for endless conversations with sensitive young thespians. He'd be much happier snoozing at the golf course.

But now, with Gus gone, his snoozing days were over —indeed, they had never started.

It was time to go outside and see how his guys were doing in today's "September Scramble." Eight teams competed in this early tournament of the season. The winner usually went on to claim the state title. For the last five years, Gus's team had done just that.

Mickey slid through the crowd and stared up at the big board on the 18th green. On it were the individual scores and the team totals. In charge, carrying a blue marker and barking orders, was Ben Flanigan, coach of the host team and minor figure in the world of high school golf. Mickey squinted up at the numbers. Earlier in the day, Forest had been trailing but moving up, but now he could see they had not caught up. In fact, the team was coming in third. Mickey turned around into a cloud of smoke and the grinning face of Coach Spalding who placed his freckled hand on his shoulder. "Well, we finally did it. We finally beat you guys. Watch out for us this year."

Mickey slipped free and made his way to his players glumly grouped by the putting green. In the middle was the captain, Peter Van Arsdale, a tall blond kid who this time next year would be playing for Duke University. "Not to worry, guys," Mickey called out cheerfully. "You played well. It wasn't our day, but this is just for practice anyway. We can talk about it on the bus."

"We're not taking the bus," Peter snapped. "My dad's driving us back in his van." Earlier Mickey had met Mr. Van Arsdale. He was a big guy with a stiff handshake and a scowl —not your typical father, as far as Mickey could tell.

So Mickey rode back alone. He didn't even bother to congratulate the other coaches. He slumped down at the front of the bus and accepted a beer from the driver. He hoped the fellow, an old-timer named Gerard, might be sympathetic. After all, how could Mickey be blamed for what his players did? What could Gus or anyone have done? But all the driver said was that Mr. Van Arsdale was a "prick with ears."

"Quit, Mickey. Quit." Shelly slid a piece of toast between Mickey and the sports page. "The guys are coaches and coaches are scumbags and that's all there is to it. Quit. We've lived together for two years, and I've never seen you look so miserable. Would you please quit? You stayed up half the night drinking. Thank God it's the weekend. Would you please quit?"

When Mickey first met Shelly at a bar, she proudly described herself as a "simple-minded bitch." No gray areas for her. Nothing lurking beneath the surface. What you see is what you get. If you were a math teacher like Mickey and taught the tough kids, you were okay. If you were a coach, forget it. She popped some more bread into the toaster. She was tall and slim and athletic-looking. She might have made a good golfer. But taking up a sport was the last thing Shelly would ever do. Graduate school and substitute teaching took all of her time.

"After the coach died," Mickey said, "I told the athletic department they could appoint someone else if they felt uncomfortable with me in charge. But the AD said I was the man and that Gus had told him I would do just fine."

"You're lying," she snapped as she smeared margarine on her toast. She sat down at the table and pushed the paper away. "The phone has started ringing. Mrs. Fleming said that before the match, you should have scheduled a team meeting to pump up the players. Mrs. Williams who incidentally has a horrible stutter, said you 'sh-sh-sh-should have p-p-played her son.' And some guy with a loud, foreign-sounding voice said that you'd 'BETTER SHAKE UP THE LINEUP' before the dual meets start. And then Tim somebody-or-other from the newspaper called, all pissed off because you forgot to phone in the scores. It won't be long until that Van Arsdale calls. Christ, what a Neanderthal he is! Mickey, do you have any idea of what you've done to yourself?"

"Look, I'll be fine. All golf coaches do is sit around. The kids all have their own pros. I just decide who plays. I make sure people show up. I go to the meetings with the other coaches. I'll figure it out. Just leave me alone." He suddenly felt very tired.

He walked into the living room and dropped down into his favorite chair. It was gray and worn, like the other used furniture that Shelly had picked up in the city. There was a pile of exams on the floor, but he wasn't going to grade them yet. There was a science fiction novel he was about to start and some old *New Yorker* issues he needed to finish, but he was too tired to read. He stared blankly at the wall and noticed that Shelly had hung up a photo of George Orwell, her favorite author. She was always doing that sort of thing—hanging things up and taking them down without ever asking. Sometimes he complained, but not today. He got up and walked outside. A bike ride would make him feel better.

Before he went into the living room to join the party, Mickey asked Mrs. Van Arsdale if he could use the bathroom. It was huge, one of the largest he had ever been in. It had two sinks, a large shower, and two dressers. Picasso prints covered two walls. Another wall was one huge mirror. Mickey stared into it. Considering the fact that he had been drinking for two days, he looked okay. His hair was sticking up and his clothes were wrinkled, but he was a teacher and that's what he was supposed to look like.

He had been asleep when the phone had rung that morning. "Mickey, this is Beth Van Arsdale, Peter's mom. Sorry to call you so early on Sunday, but Peter's dad and I want to invite you to a party we're having for the team this afternoon. It's something the captain of the team does every year. With Gus dying and all that, we forgot to ask you, but we sure hope you can come. Bring your girlfriend." Mickey said he'd be there, but he'd be coming alone. Shelly at a party with rich people wouldn't be much fun.

The living room was crowded with parents and a few school people. Mickey looked out the window and saw the golf team shooting baskets and sailing Frisbees.

Mr. Van Arsdale greeted him with a crushing handshake and led him to the bar, where he grabbed a beer and left Mickey with a couple standing nearby. Their son, along with being a good golfer, was a debating champ. "I don't suppose you've had him in class?" the wife asked.

"I don't think so," Mickey laughed. "My students are one step from dropping out."

"Special ed?" the husband asked.

"We call them 'at-risk' kids. Special ed's something else."

"It must be awfully hard work," she said.

"Not really. It's not as hard as it was when I first started."
That was true; if nothing else, he had learned how to keep
his students busy.

"I bet not many golf coaches come from that department."

"I'm the first, as far as I know."

He drank anther beer and talked for a while with Mrs.
Van Arsdale. She had been a history major at Indiana University. For two years she had taught in the city. She stood
a little too close and touched him a little too often. Once
she lowered her voice to say that the lady talking to her
husband was going through serious therapy.

Mickey was leaving the bar with his third beer when
Mr. Van Arsdale strode up and put a beefy arm around his
shoulder. "Let's go to the study."

He led Mickey into a dark room near the staircase and
gestured for him to sit on a leather couch while he stayed
standing. The room had a few bookshelves, a giant TV set,
and a desk. There were pictures on the wall of Mr. Van Arsdale and local celebrities taken at golf courses.

Mr. Van Arsdale stood over Mickey and started talking.
"My guess is that you don't like me or people like me." He
was wearing blue slacks, a yellow golf shirt, and a blue blazer. He was probably in his late fifties, but still fit-looking.

Mickey stood up and walked by the window. He could talk better standing up. "Mr. ..."

"My name's Ed."

"Mr. Van Arsdale, I don't know who you are. Why wouldn't I like you?"

"Teachers and intellectual types think rich people like me are phonies." He spoke in a low voice.

Mickey moved to the desk and leaned against it. "I never thought that at all. I thought this was a nice thing for you to do. Have a party and all that. Look, I'm a suburban brat myself. I'm not nervous around rich folks." He was pleased at how easily he could stand up to this guy.

Mr. Van Arsdale ignored him. "Is that right? Well, I'm not from the suburbs. My dad was a cop. He never went to college. I run a factory in the city. I've got a scar on my back where a Puerto Rican stabbed me. I might be a college grad and a member of a country club, but that's only part of the story—and not the interesting part either."

Mickey shrugged. He figured Mr. Van Arsdale wouldn't like a shrug.

"You know, kid, there's more to the job than you might think."

"I know that." He knew what was coming.

"You really don't know anything—if you excuse my frankness. Sure, a golf coach is not a golf pro. He wouldn't dare tell a kid how to swing. But the coach does things. He has choices. Gus made all the right ones. He started his recruiting with seventh graders. When he spotted a good young golfer, he'd make sure the kid came to Forest and not to St. Regis and not to a prep school. He schmoozed the parents so that would happen. A lot of golfers go away. Or they might decide to play football or soccer."

"That makes sense," Mickey yawned.

"And he worked with the kids. If they played poorly, he knew what to say. If they played well, he knew what to say. If they were peaking and slumping, he knew what to say. He could talk to parents. He could talk to the golf pros."

"I can learn to do all of that."

"He was great at finding scholarships for the kids. He knew the college people. They all wanted Gus's kids to play for them. Surprised?"

Mickey was determined not to let this guy bully him. He raised his voice and looked the man in the eye. "Give me some credit. I knew it was a big job. You don't need to talk down to me."

"People thought that just because Gus was a driver's ed teacher that he was a second-rate guy, but he wasn't. Did you know he was an orphan? He wasn't from golfing culture." This guy was obviously used to getting his way. He dealt with union people and contractors and tough guys all the time. These people in the suburbs were nothing. And teachers like Mickey were as weak as they come.

"I want you to give the job to someone else. My oldest son has time. He works for me at the factory, but he could take off in the afternoon. He knows what to do. You have no idea what you're doing. The kids won't respect you. They think you're an imposter. Believe me, they do. You can't play golf. You don't have any connections. You will make the job meaningless. Kids will go out for other sports. They won't try. Do you get the idea?"

Maybe it was the booze, but Mickey didn't feel the least bit intimidated by this guy. He looked back and told him what he didn't want to hear. "I'm not going to quit. I was hired. I'll do my best. They can fire me next year, but this year I want the job." Then he headed for the door. "I'm going home now. Thanks for the beer."

He strode back into the living room. By now the kids were eating a cake shaped like a putting green. Mickey walked over to the bar and poured himself a shot of scotch. He threw it down and then walked over to Mrs. Van Arsdale, who was chatting with two newcomers. "I have to go now, Mrs. V. Thanks for the hospitality." He gave her shoulder a hug, the way his parents used to do with their friends. "I hope all you parents keep supporting the team." At the door, he looked back at the kids who were still stuffing their faces. "OK, guys. See you at the course tomorrow. We've got work to do."

In the driveway, Mr. Van Arsdale caught up with him. He had replaced his blazer with a sweatshirt. "Mickey, wait a second. I've changed my mind. You've obviously got more balls than I thought. You should do just fine. I misread you. Let's have one more drink. I'll take you to my favorite bar. I'm getting sick of these suburban types." He slid into the seat next to Mickey and told him to drive toward Skokie.

Jilly's Place was small and dark. Mr. Van Arsdale shouted a hello to two construction workers at the bar. They were watching the Bears game on the TV. He nodded to a red-haired guy sitting alone in a booth along the side and reading a Tom Clancy novel. He gestured for Mickey to sit down at a table in the middle. He went to the bar to order two tequilas. He came back with the drinks along with a lime and salt.

As they sat drinking, Mickey did most of the talking. He told Mr. Van Arsdale that he had gone to college in the West and taught in Seattle. Two years ago he had moved to the Midwest to go to graduate school at Northwestern. His father was a lawyer; his mom sold real estate. His sister ran a day-care center. One day he hoped to write a novel.

Mr. Van Arsdale got up and ordered more drinks. When he got back, Mickey started talking about teaching. He said that his current job—working with the problem kids in math—was not his first choice, but a job is a job and he was pretty good at it. Mr. Van Arsdale said that he'd hate to spend his life helping losers. "I'd flatten them the first chance I had." Mickey shrugged and finished the second drink. He had forgotten how much he liked tequila.

Mr. Van Arsdale went back to the bar for two more. On the way, he stopped by the side booth to joke with the red-haired man.

By the time Mickey finished the third drink, his head was spinning a little and he was starting to slur his words.

It was dark in the parking lot when Mickey climbed into

his Ford. He was alone. Mr. Van Arsdale had ridden home with someone from Jilly's. "No point for you to drive out of your way, Mickey." The two agreed to talk early the next week. Mr. Van Arsdale had some material from Gus that Mickey would need.

Maybe Shelly would be up for a movie. He didn't feel like fighting with her. He'd play down his success with Mr. Van Arsdale. He'd agree with her that he'd taken the job for the wrong reason, but now he kind of liked it. He was looking for something outside of school. Balance was what he needed. Balance. He would make friends with some of these kids; he didn't always need to be with burnouts and sluts.

He started the car and turned on the radio just in time to hear the Bears lose to the 49ers, 17–16. A field goal attempt on the final play had fallen short. He smoked a cigarette and fished around in a bag on the floor for an old Rolling Stones CD. It was the one with "Beast of Burden," one of his all-time favorite songs. He found it and slipped it into the player and listened to Mick Jagger.

He had been driving for only a few blocks when the police car sped up behind him with its lights flashing. He knew enough to stay put. Cops get very edgy if you get out.

Through the rearview mirror, he could see the officer in his car talking on his cell phone. Then he wrote something down, got out of his car, and walked toward Mickey. He stopped halfway to copy down Mickey's license plate number and started walking again. He was dressed in cop blue trousers, blue shirt, dark blue tie, and a blue hat perched on top of his red hair.

Bud
Comes Back

"So you were a student here at one time, and now you're back to paint this shithole." He nodded up to the building near to where they were sitting on the lawn. "Must feel odd." Floyd stopped gabbing and chomped down on his ham sandwich. A tiny puddle of mayonnaise collected on his lip. "Couldn't have been that long ago. You still look young."

Bud shrugged. "Older than I look. But not much." He had always looked young, and even being locked up hadn't changed that.

"What year did you graduate?" Floyd was working on the crust now.

"My class graduated in 2000. I left before."

"GED?"

"My counselor said that was the best plan. If I'd stayed in school, it would've taken me forever to graduate."

"I'm thinking about getting a GED." Floyd reached into his breast pocket for a cigarette.

Bud nodded. "You might as well." He had met Floyd that morning. Floyd had worked on the crew for several years. He was one of those guys who knew everything. The kind of asshole Bud tried to avoid. But no one seemed to like Floyd, and that's why he was eating alone and had gestured for Bud to join him on the lawn in front of the school.

It was summer school, and the place felt empty. Not many kids. Not many teachers. Bud ate half a chicken sandwich and then watched Floyd wipe his mouth with his sleeve and start sipping from a brown bag. "Wouldn't want to get caught drinking on school property." His eyes glistened, and his lips trembled. He was a big, flabby guy. Wouldn't last long in prison, including the boot-camp prison Bud had been in.

Floyd put down the bag. "What else have you been doing?" There was a stupid grin. He knew just what Bud had been doing. He wanted to hear all about it. Well, too bad.

Bud stood up abruptly. "I'm going to paint. See you tomorrow." He walked back into the building and headed for Room 212.

This was Bud's first job since getting out, and, once he got into it, he wouldn't feel edgy and that's all that mattered now. Get on with it. The more he worked, the easier to forget boot camp.

How the fuck could that be a "humane alternative" to prison? He'd rather have been behind bars instead of that freezing barrack with the thugs and the sadistic guards and the scared-straight bullshit. The guy in the bunk across from him was huge and stupid. ("See these hands? I used these to strangle my boyfriend, and you might be next, white boy.")

The first thing Bud did was push the desks into the middle of the classroom and cover them with a tarp. Then he reached into his pocket for the scraper and went to work on the peeling green paint under the chalkboard behind the desk.

Mr. Gabriel had sat on top of that desk when he taught American Literature. He was in his forties. He acted smart enough, but this had been his first time with the so-called "non-accelerated group." Below average is what they were. No real fuckups, but no Einsteins either. Most were quite agreeable. They sat near the front and nodded and did the right thing. They were headed for shitty colleges and shitty jobs and that was fine. Nothing wrong with being harmless. Bud, Ned, and Herb had sat in the back and tipped their desks. They smirked and muttered. When Bud got to class —usually late—and ambled to the back row, the weenies in the front would stare at him nervously. He liked that.

Up until that class, it had never occurred to Bud to act tough. He wasn't tough, so why act that way? But with this group, he could be a hard guy and get away with it. In the halls and on the streets, it was a different story.

While Bud would entertain his buddies with muttered comments, Mr. G. spent his time with the agreeables. He'd ask them obvious questions about the books and they would answer or almost answer and that would fill the time. Sometimes he'd call on the back-row crowd, and they would grin and pretend not to hear. Every once in a while they would say something clever, and Mr. G. would be all over them with compliments.

One time after class, Mr. G. stopped Bud and talked about potential. He was like some eager teacher in a corny movie trying to get through to his reluctant learners. He looked Bud in the eye and actually said, "You have potential, Bud. Give yourself a chance. Let's go have a cup of coffee and we can look at your papers."

Bud shrugged. He figured that Mr. G. was probably a fag. He also figured he was bored with the agreeables and wanted some variety. It looked good to reach out to the rough kids. The trouble was that Bud wasn't really tough, and Mr. G. was not really interested.

What a strange job! You spend all your time with kids who don't give a shit. No one really knows when you do a good job. And people are watching you all the time. That's what Bud wouldn't like—being watched all the time. At boot camp he was always being watched. Watched by the guards and by the other prisoners.

The funny thing was that in boot camp, he was agreeable. He minded his own business. He lived in a barrack and did work all day long. But you could get really hurt if you pissed off the wrong people.

Bud took a writing class at boot camp. He did all right, but the teacher, a good-looking lady with no makeup, kept trying too much to get them to tell about their lives. It was not that bitch's business. Maybe she was going to write a book about it or something. Plus she acted relaxed, but you could see her hands shaking a little. And she'd hurry out when class was over.

He scraped for the rest of the day.

The next day he had just started scraping again when through the door walked Mr. Gabriel.

"Hello, Bud." He was wearing a jogging suit and carrying a tennis racquet. He looked like someone on the cover of a travel magazine. "I've seen you around and wanted to say hello."

Bud stood up and actually crossed the room to shake his hand. "I recognized you, too. I'm surprised you're teaching summer school."

"I like to teach. This is what I do. I'm done by noon. I ride my bike and play tennis. It's a good life."

Bud looked around. "It's been a long time."

"Not that long—only eight years or so. I'm still here. Fifty years old." He stopped talking and walked over and touched Bud on the arm. "I hear you've had a hard time." He put the racquet on the desk and moved over to the window and leaned against the ledge. "You had some trouble with the law."

"After I quit school, I worked at a restaurant and then got laid off. I decided to make some money so I could move. I was caught selling weed to an undercover cop. It wasn't much. They wanted to make an example of me, and the only help I had was from a public defender who didn't know anything. They sent me to one of those jail boot camps."

"Is that what they call a shock facility?" Mr. G. seemed quite interested.

"That's what they call them," Bud answered quietly.

"Were you shocked?"

He smiled, and Bud snapped, "Yeah, I was shocked. But I wasn't raped. Isn't that what you guys want to know?"

Instead of saying anything, Mr. G. just stood there, half-smiling and tilting his head. Finally he spoke. "'You guys'?" He backed away but kept his eyes on Bud. "'You guys'?"

"You know what I mean."

"You mean a gay person? A homosexual? A faggot? A

poof? A Nancy boy? Light in the loafers? Limp wristed? Is that what you mean?" He didn't raise his voice, but he spoke clearly. He wanted Bud to hear the words. He wanted to embarrass him.

Bud stood silently, staring at the floor. He should have kept his mouth shut.

When he looked up, Mr. G. was gone. Bud was no longer angry. But he wasn't sad either. Or guilty. He didn't know what to feel.

The truth was he hadn't been raped, but he might as well have been. Omar, the guy in the next bunk at boot camp, told him all about it. He had been raped in a county jail. Ten guys had held him down. "Each one of them fucked me in the ass." He bled all over. He'd never slept much since. "If you go to prison, especially if you're a small white guy, you'll get it in the ass; be ready."

That night Bud and his dad watched a ball game together on TV. His mom had died when Bud was in eighth grade. His dad, who had taken early retirement from the phone company, watched TV all day long. After Bud was released, he let him come home, but he never really talked to him. He was a cold, unforgiving man.

"How was work?" the old man asked in a flat voice.

"Work was okay. I scraped and painted my old classroom. I ran into my old English teacher."

"Who's that?"

"Mr. Gabriel."

"Gay guy, right?"

"I wouldn't know."

The next day Mr. G. stopped in Room 212 at the same time. By now Bud had started painting.

He looked up at his old teacher. "I'm sorry about yesterday." It seemed like the right thing to say. Somehow the man didn't deserve the abuse.

"I'm not sorry." Mr. G. walked over and leaned against the window ledge.

Bud put the paintbrush down and stood up.

"I'm not sorry because you meant it. And yes, I am gay and proud of it. No one cares around here." He waited for a few seconds and then continued. "Do you remember when I asked you to come in?"

"Yeah, I guess."

"I wanted you to understand why I liked your writing. That was all. You said no and laughed and walked off. Later,

I was walking down the hall and I saw you imitating me. You were putting on a show for your friends. And, I must say, you were quite funny. You nailed me. I was a silly idealist trying to get through to kids who despised school."

Bud remembered the moment. His friends had actually applauded. "I'm sorry. That was a lousy thing to do."

"Don't be sorry. But do you know what happened right there in the hallway while you were putting on your little show?"

Bud shook his head. He wasn't going to say anything.

"I decided right then to worry about other students. I was changing anyway, but your little performance did it. The tipping point. I stopped playing the role and became what I am now. And you did it. I learned to ignore people like you. You were not my style.

"So, that's what I learned. How about you? Did boot camp teach you to be tough? You weren't tough when I knew you."

Bud ignored his questions and spoke in a low voice, staring out the window behind Mr. G. "So, you've had it with losers. No point in sucking up to kids that don't give a shit. No point in pretending they have more than they really do. Is that it?"

Mr. G. smiled broadly. "Well put, Bud. But one more thing. When I said you had something, I meant it. Next to your deadbeat friends and those agreeable bores, you stood out. So I meant what I said. And your papers did show promise. You were much more honest in writing than you were in class. "

"But that was then."

"That was then. Anyway, paint the room well. I'll be teaching here in the fall."

Freddy's Place

We always enjoyed watching Freddy arrive at work. Someone would say, "Here he comes," and we'd crowd over to the window as the city bus pulled up, and out the door came this tallish, chubby Forest High School kid, with a goofy smile and a nerdy T-shirt. He'd saunter across the lawn past the garden and into the library. It's not like he was a freak or something, but he was just different enough to get our attention. There were four of us—all semiretired library workers. We shelved books and answered questions, but we had time to see what was happening.

We just really liked this young man. How could you not like a high school kid who showed up for work right when he was supposed to? He even had his own key because he liked to work late. He listened. He helped. He smiled. He wasn't at all like those rude young people who smirked behind your back.

Part of the time, Freddy helped out Leroy, our custodian. Freddy would wax the floor, change lightbulbs, and do other work like that. He even mowed the lawn. He could fix a toilet. He knew how to set up the big room for special events. He was also in charge of getting the biography section back to where it should be. He put the books in alphabetical order according to subject. He erased pencil marks. He taped torn pages. He got rid of biographies that were beyond repair, and he even placed some orders. He shelved biographies that had been donated by local rich people.

Freddy obviously thought about what he was doing because he told several of us how amazing it was that some people could be important enough to have books written about them. When he said it, it was like he was talking to himself.

Young people who work at our library usually have lunch down the street at McDonald's. But Freddy ate with the library staff. He even called us by our first names. He joked about the Cubs and the other loser Chicago teams. He'd ask questions about local events, like the 1968 Democratic Convention, that had happened before he was born. He even enjoyed making fun of himself as an athlete. His classmates said he "threw like a girl."

Another reason we cared so much for Freddy was that he had had so much sadness in his life. His older brother had gone to jail for selling drugs. After that, Freddy's parents, who were old and crabby to begin with, just gave up and sat around bewildered and let the house go to seed. Then his dad lost his job with Peabody Insurance. His mom, who was always a little odd, turned even meaner. They were just plain disagreeable people. And living with them must have been depressing.

Freddy started working at the library the summer right after his brother was taken away. Our assistant librarian,

Jake Wentz, knew the family and the situation and offered him the job. And Freddy took it.

He didn't seem to care much about things that most high school kids cared about. From what we could tell, he had only a few friends. They would stop by the library, and they had the same harmless look as Freddy. One of the other librarians lived near him and said he didn't go out much. And a teacher we all knew from Forest High said he was the utter opposite of his brother. No booze or drugs. No wild parties. No fast driving. He always dressed kind of simple —usually T-shirts with pictures of famous people like Einstein. He wore his hair in a ponytail.

One time at lunch he told us that he had recently visited his brother in prison. He said his brother was in with some hard cases. Murderers and rapists. It was ridiculous, he said, for his brother to be there at all, but especially with such dangerous people. Then he stood up and walked off. That was the last time we talked about his brother.

He was always nice to all of us, so we weren't surprised that he was nice to this older lady who started hanging around the library. She wasn't exactly a bag lady, but she came pretty close. She wore heavy clothes even in the summer. She had straggly red hair. Someone said she looked like an old Orphan Annie. And she had bags and sat on the bench in front of the library.

One morning when she was sitting on the bench, Freddy walked by and she called out to him—something about him looking like a weenie. It sounded insulting to us. Who wants to be called a weenie? But he laughed and went over and they talked for a while, and then he went inside and downstairs to his biographies.

She came back practically every day, and Freddy always found time for her. She was usually on the bench or somewhere nearby and they would chat. They always laughed a lot. It was kind of cute—but not surprising. A decent fellow like Freddy would take an interest in an old needy person. Isn't that what decent people do?

He told us that she was from Seattle. Her name was Brenda. Someone in her family had cheated her out of all of her money. She had come to the Midwest to live in a building owned by her nephew. Her room was tiny and gloomy and that's why she came to the library. She brought her bags with her because she was sure someone in the building would steal them if she left them behind. When the weather got colder, she'd be going south. Her nephew had a place outside of Tampa.

Of course, we wanted to know what they talked about. Freddy shrugged and said, "Not much." But then he said that she liked to ask him questions: What did he do in school? What did he like about it? What did he hate? What makes kids angry? And they talked about current events and old TV shows.

"What about Brenda?" we asked. "What does she have to say?"

"Oh," he answered, "whatever she feels like." We wanted to hear more, but it wasn't surprising that Freddy would respect her privacy. Most young people wouldn't give a hoot about Brenda's privacy. But Freddy did.

He kept on meeting her all through the summer. We figured he was too nice a kid to turn her away. And besides, he might be looking for more adult company. He certainly didn't get any at his own house. He still worked hard; he still was pleasant to us. He just added this friendship to his life at the library.

No doubt about it, Brenda was happier because she had made contact with this young man. She always wore her hair tied back with a string and wore winter clothes and had a little limp when she walked, but she smiled a lot. And we figured Freddy had a lot to do with that smile.

But she didn't smile when Arlo Simmons, our head librarian, came around. At first he had ignored her. Then one afternoon he stopped by the bench where they were talking. He said something to her and then she smirked, and he said something to Freddy, who just stared back at him. It was pretty obvious to us that Simmons had not wanted Freddy to talk to her. Of course, Simmons couldn't very well send Brenda away. This was a public library. How would it look if the head librarian banished a homeless person?

Once school started up in the fall, Freddy cut back on his library work. He had four classes at Forest High, plus an independent study with a younger teacher who had started at Forest High the year before. We asked him what it was about. He said he would tell us when he had more time, but he really didn't have much time and we really didn't care that much.

But we still saw him on Mondays and Thursdays and weekends. He had more to do away from work and sometimes didn't seem quite as jolly, but that was okay. He still had plenty of time to chat with Brenda. Once, he took her to the restaurant across the street.

Simmons had left her alone for a while, but in October,

when she started coming inside more, he started to harass her. He never kicked her out, but we often saw him next to her at the table doing a lot of talking. She would snicker and that must have made him mad.

Freddy stayed away from this, but one afternoon he stopped Simmons in the lobby and they had words. As usual, Simmons was wearing a suit and Freddy was in a tie-dyed shirt. No one heard a word of what they were saying. But we were quite sure Simmons was talking about Brenda. What else could it be? And Freddy was almost certainly defending her. And Simmons would not like that at all.

About that time, we heard from our friend at Forest High that Freddy was having some problems. Apparently in the hall after school, another student had said something nasty to Freddy about his brother. Freddy walked up and hit the boy in the mouth. It turned out that this boy was not quite right to begin with. So you can imagine students passing the word that the drug dealer's brother had attacked a special ed student. There was going to be some kind of hearing in two weeks.

Then Freddy's neighbor told us that there had been a police car in front of Freddy's house. Maybe the family of the boy Freddy hit was pressing charges or something.

Apparently Freddy's father had walked out to the car with the officers. He didn't look good. People were wondering if he had started drinking.

And then Freddy was gone.

He stopped coming to work. He stopped going to school. His neighbor said that more cops came by, but now they were talking to people in the neighborhood to see if anyone had seen Freddy. The family car was missing.

There was something in the paper. His English teacher from Forest High said he was a good kid, but this year he had turned more argumentative. Freddy's parents left the house more. The mom actually looked more capable than she had the last time we saw her.

Simmons called a meeting about Freddy. He looked concerned. He said that if we had any idea where Freddy might be, we should let him know. He really looked anxious. And then—and this is really incredible—he asked Brenda to come in, and she said that Freddy had been really depressed the last time they talked. But he had told her that if he disappeared not to worry because he knew of a safe place to live. And she said she was leaving for the south to live in her nephew's place.

We still had not seen Freddy, but we weren't really worried. We figured Freddy could take care of himself.

Then, a week later, Jake called a meeting first thing in the morning. Only the four of us were there. Simmons was off at a meeting in Boston. The purpose, Jake said, was to show us what he had found in the basement of the library.

We followed him downstairs, past the biographies, past another row of miscellaneous books and old magazines, to a door that was usually locked. It was a storeroom. Most of us had never been in it. We weren't sure we even remembered there was a door there.

He opened the door and we walked into a small, dark space about the size of an elevator—one of those larger ones that are used for freight. A bare bulb hung from the ceiling. Jake turned on the bulb and light filled the space, and we could see that we were in what must have been Freddy's place.

Along the far wall was a long table and a chair where he must have sat. It was an old wooden table with a cracked leg held tight with gray duct tape. It must have been moved down from the reference room years ago. The folding chair was like many others the library uses for events. There was a coffee cup filled with pencils and pens, mostly the blue and yellow ones from our library. There was a small stack of legal pads. There was an old computer and some reference books. There was a small fan. Underneath was a big box with more paper. On the wall over the desk was a quote from Abbie Hoffman:

I believe in compulsory cannibalism. If people were forced to eat what they killed, there would be no more wars.

On the right was a small pile of books. Jake picked them up one by one and read each title: *Soul on Ice* by Eldridge Cleaver, *Steal This Book* by Abbie Hoffman, *Death at an Early Age* by Jonathan Kozol, and *Howl and Other Poems* by Alan Ginsberg.

"This is all from the sixties—flower children, hippies, protestors," Jake said. "It looks like some pages are marked and there are some notes." Taped on the wall were articles about the Occupy movement. Jake looked up at us. "Freddy was definitely following things carefully.

"And look at this." Jake pointed to a stack of articles in the far corner. "These are all about Brenda. Her last name is Hogan. She'd been married to an old radical from the University of Washington. He had lost his job. Then he died.

Brenda had been arrested for writing threatening letters. One letter celebrated what happened to the Twin Towers on 9/11. She sent it to the Seattle newspaper. America had it coming, according to her."

We just stood there, staring. Finally, Jake spoke up again, "What I can't decide is whether Freddy did this just to kill time, or if he was really serious, or maybe both. And did Brenda give him the idea? Did she help him out? Did they spend much time here?" He was shaking his head and looking down at his feet. He was obviously bothered by this more than we were. But, of course, it had been his idea to hire Freddy in the first place.

We were silent again. Finally, Jake said softly that we'd better do something about the room before Simmons got back from Boston. A couple of us volunteered to help Leroy clean it out.

And that was that. Freddy might come back or he might stay away. He might get his name in the paper for doing something. Or he might be an unknown person, like most of us. Whatever he did, we'd understand. He was one of us. Still, before we started to clean up, Jake snapped a picture of Freddy's place. "Just in case," he muttered as he put the phone back into his pocket. "Just in case."

About the Author

Bob Boone started teaching in 1964. He has taught in Staten Island, Germany, Highland Park, and Chicago. In 1991, he founded Young Chicago Authors to provide opportunities for young writers from the city.

He has written several textbooks, a teaching memoir, and a sports biography. With Mark Henry Larson, he has coauthored three creative writing books. *Forest High* is his first work of fiction, and *Back to Forest High* is his second.

He lives in Glencoe, Illinois, with his wife Sue. He has three children and five grandchildren.

Made in the USA
San Bernardino, CA
15 November 2015